FOX
Part I

FOX
Part I

Brian Shakespeare

Based on a series for television written by Trevor Preston

NEW ENGLISH LIBRARY/TIMES MIRROR

A New English Library Original Publication, 1980

First NEL Paperback Edition February 1980

NEL Books are published by
New English Library from
Barnard's Inn, Holborn,
London EC1N 2JR.
Made and printed in Great Britain by
William Collins Sons & Co Ltd
Glasgow

45004776 8

ONE

IT was a special morning. Billy was the first of the Fox family up, as usual. He sluiced himself, army style, in the small, neatly laid-out bathroom. Head, neck and shoulders dripping, he looked at himself in the wall mirror. Seventy years old today, he thought. I've got my own teeth, full head of hair, a straight back and I hope my heart's still in the right place. Can't be too bad. He wiped the water off with the towel from around his waist. As he turned he saw on his back in the mirror the multicoloured fox tattoo which seemed to move with his body. Well, he thought, I may have been a flash bastard in my time but there's never been anything wrong with a bit of fun when it don't hurt no one.

Ray Fox, the second of Billy's sons, was still up. Nearly forty, good-looking but hard, he was leaving his West End club after an all-night card game. Ray stalled the two faces with him who'd done well and wanted more action. Tonight was the big party for Billy. When Ray reached the white Jaguar parked in a side street his face clouded. Some comedian had neatly placed a line of empty beer cans along the roof. 'Germs,' he said to himself. He swept the cans on to the road, got in the car and drove off with a squeal of tyres.

Billy Fox walked out into the back garden of his terraced house near Clapham Common. This is the best time of the day, he thought. Blue sky, not a cloud. It's going to be a lovely spring day. His suit as neat and tended as his garden, Billy walked round the small plot checking every plant and flower. Here and there he leaned over to smell a bloom, finally stopped to pick one and put it in his button-hole.

Not far away on Clapham Common Kenny Fox, the youngest of Billy's sons, was on his early morning run. A good-looking boy of twenty-one, he jogged between his manager, Eddie Chapman, and Chalky, a useful light heavy. Wearing a tracksuit, woollen hat, and a sweat towel round his neck, already his young face bore the marks and scars that said he was a fighter. As the early traffic passed across the Common, a car slowed beside them for the driver to shout a word of greeting. Kenny gave the fan a brief wave, without losing his rhythm.

'Sweat 'im, Eddie,' the fan called. 'Got a ton on that boy at two to one.'

Eddie slowed. 'Two to one?'

' 'S right.'

Kenny turned towards the fan. 'Robbery,' he grunted, and ran on.

Billy Fox strode through the manor like a monarch surveying his kingdom. Everywhere passers-by waved, sometimes stopped for a word. As he turned a corner he nearly collided with a clippie in uniform, on her way to the garage to pick up her bus.

'Happy birthday, Billy,' she said. ' 'Ere, give us a kiss.' She reached up and gave him a big hug. Billy gave her bottom a friendly squeeze.

'How's yer love life, Rosie?'

'All he thinks about is Fulham getting promoted,' she giggled.

'What a wicked waste.'

Rose checked the man's watch on his wrist. 'Got to shoot, love. Buy you a birthday drink in the Crown later?'

'Tata.' Billy walked on down the street to the newsagent. Inside the shop Kipper, frail and in his fifties, one of the lenses of his glasses blacked out, was sorting the papers to send with the delivery boy.

'Billy! Bin waitin' for yer. Happy birthday, you old tyke.'

'Not so much of the old.'

'You don't look a day over sixty-nine,' said Kipper solemnly.

'You saucy sod!'

' 'Ang about.'

Kipper walked into the living quarters behind the shop. The rat-faced delivery boy put out a hand to swipe a packet of cigarettes. He thought Billy, his back turned, couldn't see.

'He's only blind in one eye,' said Billy, turning slowly.

'I wan' doin' nothin'.' The kid froze.

'If you weren't doin' *nothin'*, you must've been doin' *somethin'*. Elementary grammar.'

'I wan' . . .' the boy started to protest.

'You got to thieve, thieve from them that can afford it,' Billy said, giving him a look. The boy moved quickly away and stuffed the marked papers into his bag before Kipper returned. He had a present, wrapped in green tissue paper, in his hand.

'Marge did the wrappin',' Kipper said, holding out the package. He turned to the delivery boy, standing by the door with his papers. 'Don't you go bitin' that dog again.'

' 'E bit me!' the boy protested, leaving the shop.

'Nearly 'ad its rotten ear off he did,' Kipper said to Billy, who smiled. Billy read the little greetings card on top of his present, very moved.

'Ain't you goin' to open it?'

'Don't quite know what to say, Kip.'

'Billy Fox short on words. Never!'

Billy tore the wrapping to find a box of fine Havana cigars.

'Now that's what you call a real smoke.'

'Best Havana,' said Kipper.

'Did you know the Cuban women who make 'em roll them on their thighs?'

'Go on?'

'Right up near their lunch box,' Billy nodded. 'That's why they're so smooth.'

Vin, the eldest of the five Fox brothers, lived with his wife and three kids in a large Victorian house in Battersea. It had a big back garden, a bit wild but marvellous for the children. The two girls were no problem but his younger son, nine-year-old Andy, had been profoundly deaf from birth.

On the morning of Billy's birthday, Vin was out early with Andy by the pond at the end of the garden. Andy, wearing a hearing aid, was feeding the fish. With infinite patience Vin was teaching the boy to lip read. Vin touched his son on the shoulder. Andy turned towards him.

'They're full,' Vin patted his stomach. 'Full up.' Andy concentrated on Vin's mouth, pointed to the fish and tried to speak. All that came out was a strange nasal sound. Vin squatted beside Andy so that their faces were on a level.

'Ffffisshh,' he enunciated carefully.

'Fffwww . . . fffwwwiii,' Andy tried his best.

'Fish . . . fishhh.'

'Ffffiizzzhh,' Andy tried stubbornly.

Vin gave Andy a thumbs up, scooped him up playfully to throw him in the air.

'It won't be for the want of tryin', will it, son?'

Billy Fox walked back over Clapham Common, box of cigars in his hand. Kenny, Eddie and Chalky were finishing their run and veered towards him.

'Happy birthday, Pop,' Kenny called.

'Happy birthday, Billy,' Eddie panted. He was a health freak but at forty-five couldn't compete with the two fighters.

'Seventy?' Chalky shouted. 'He don't even look sixty.'

'He could still go ten rounds,' Kenny nodded.

'Fifteen,' Billy said, breaking into a run beside them. He turned to Eddie. 'How's he shaping up, Eddie?'

'A real prospect.' He smiled at Kenny. 'He might go three if he gets lucky.'

Kenny turned fast, ran backwards and let go half a dozen lethal punches at Eddie, pulling them just short of the body.

'Well, maybe four,' Eddie corrected himself.

Billy laughed, stopped running. 'See yer later.'

'Don't get into any trouble,' Kenny called.

'Do I ever?'

Back at Billy's house, his wife Connie was still asleep when he came in with a tray of tea and biscuits. On the tray he'd put the flower he'd picked for his button-hole, in a small glass. At fifty-three, Connie was still an attractive woman. Billy put the tray on the bedside table and gently shook her shoulder.

'Connie. Connie, love. You wanted to get to Vin's by nine.'

Connie stirred, saw the tea and the flower, sat up.

'You're a lovely man,' she said, taking Billy in her arms and kissing him. 'Happy birthday, love!' She kissed him again and Billy gently eased away.

'Any more of that an' I'll be slippin' back in with yer.'

Connie threw back the bedclothes to challenge him. 'Come on then.'

'After last night!' He laughed. 'I'm officially an old man now.'

'You'll *never* be old, Billy Fox.'

*

Joey Fox, thirty-four, was the brother who definitely had a way with the ladies. Good-looking and cheeky with it, he knew he could pull almost any bird he fancied. Driving along the Bayswater Road that morning, two City types hailed his London black. He pulled into the kerb, listening in pained disbelief while they argued whose cab it was. Tired of the confrontation, Joey slipped into gear and accelerated a few yards up the street to pick up a pretty girl, also looking for a cab. As she got in Joey gave her one of his special smiles.

'I'm all yours, sweetheart,' he said.

The City men gawped, motionless, as the taxi moved away up the street.

Billy stopped his car at Vin's front door to a very enthusiastic reception as the kids came steaming out of the house. The girls, Sammy and Karen, and little Andy all shouted their birthday greetings, squealing with excitement. Andy competed with the girls to swing up in Billy's arms. Then a white Mini pulled into the drive, and the three kids dragged Billy over to say hello to Nan, Kenny's long-standing girlfriend. Nan, nineteen and very pretty, got out of her car to the same welcome from the kids while Connie and Vin's wife, Renie, looked on laughing.

'Happy birthday, Billy,' said Nan, giving him a kiss on the cheek.

'What d'yer call that?' Billy pointed to his cheek. 'I want a real splonker.'

Nan giggled and gave Billy another, longer kiss.

'That's more like it.'

Andy jumped up, clamped his hands around Billy's neck and gave him an enormous kiss.

'You show 'em how it's done, Andy boy,' Billy said approvingly while Nan went over to greet Connie and Renie. Nan turned back to Billy.

'Did you see Kenny this morning?'

'Course, every mornin'.' Billy winked at Connie and Renie. 'He was looking a bit tired. What you bin doin' to 'im?'

Nan blushed.

'Billy Fox . . . *behave!*' Connie said, laughing.

Phil Fox made his way through the sprawling grounds of the red-brick university, holdall in his hand. Long-haired, serious-faced, at twenty-six he was a postgraduate student and the acknowledged 'intellectual' in the family. He took a lot of jokes but he knew that his brothers admired him for it. He was thinking about the party that night for Billy when a smart new car pulled up beside him with a toot on the horn. Phil turned to see an attractive girl, casually but expensively dressed, leaning out of the window.

'You must be Anna?'

'David said you wanted a lift to London.' Anna's voice was a touch pound note.

'If you've got a spare seat.'

'I think I can squeeze you in.' Anna gestured round the empty car.

In a few minutes they were on the London road and Phil had time to give her an appreciative once over as well as to see that she drove fast and confidently.

'Dave said you'd be with your bloke.'

'He's gone to Yorkshire to see his parents.' Her tone was non-committal.

'We've met before, haven't we?'

She looked at him. 'At David's party. We had . . . words.'

'Oh dear.' Phil felt uneasy. 'What sort of words?'

'You were doing the "last of the working class heroes" act.' Anna paused. 'You told me I was, now let me get this verbatim, a spoiled middle class cow with . . .'

Now Phil remembered. 'A voice like a wet paper bag,' he completed the sentence, embarrassed.

'I thought you were too pissed to remember anything but the first verse of the Red Flag. You fell down the stairs.'

Phil pretended to open the car door. 'Shall I get out now?'

Anna dropped down a gear, accelerating into a tight bend, tyres squealing. 'That's up to you. I'm not stopping.'

Vin drove into the yard of his scaffold business to find his work-force of three loading up a lorry with pipes, clamps and boards. They waved as he parked by his office and Vin called out to Clem to join him inside. Vin sat down at his cramped desk and glanced through the mail.

'Where's Vera?'

'At the dentist,' Clem said.

'Oh yeah.' He paused a moment. 'Something's come up. I

wanted a quiet word with you.'

Vin took out a packet of cigarettes, offered one to Clem, then went on, 'I had the foreman from that site in Crawley on to me this mornin'. A brand new Kango and set of chisels, two hundred quid's worth, have gone for a walk. He was makin' nasty noises.'

'It weren't none of our lads, Vin. No way. If that snakey little bastard is tryin' to put it on us, he's givin' you a load of old fanny. Dirty little slag!'

'Easy, Clem,' Vin said quietly.

Clem counted on his fingers. 'There was me, Ben and Harry. And Willie on that Sat'day. We all arrived in the lorry an' left in it. I'd've seen if anythink 'ad been loaded on that lorry. Specially somethin' the size of a bleedin' Kango!'

'I'm going down to see 'im this mornin',' Vin said.

'I'll come with yer,' Clem said quickly.

'No you won't.'

'Why not, guvnor?'

'You know why. You're too fast with your hands.' Vin gave Clem a hard stare. 'If he's tryin' it on he's going to come unstuck.'

Joey Fox dropped his last customer of the morning at Victoria Station. It couldn't have worked out better, since he'd arranged to meet his mate Griff at the cabbies' noshery round the corner in Ebury Street. He parked, jumped out with his leather money bag and whistled to himself as he walked down the street. Crossing the island triangle, he suddenly saw Liz leave the little restaurant. He darted down the steps of the street lavatory to hide. Liz had turned out to be a big mistake, he thought, while he gave her a couple of minutes to get away. He came up the steps very slowly, checking he was clear, then nipped across the road.

Inside it was crowded as usual, full of cabbies tucking into monster plates of food, chatting away or reading trade papers like *Cab Trade News* or *Steering Wheel*. Griff had kept a seat near the corner and waved as Joey came over.

'Jesus, Joey, you just missed Laughin' Lil!'

'I know, I saw her leaving.'

'I thought you said you'd knocked it on the 'ead with that number,' Griff said in exasperation.

'I have. But she won't bloody listen. I told 'er . . . told her straight, didn' I?'

'That's not her version.'

'You know her.'

'I know *you*,' Griff pointed accusingly.

'Oh that's nice. I mean, that's charmin'. I was in a good mood'n'all.' Joey picked up a menu, pretended to study it.

'She wants to see you.'

'I need to see that lady like I need another 'ole in me arse.'

Griff interrupted. 'She's in a right state, Joey.'

'Neurotic!' Joey exclaimed. 'No wonder her 'ole man works away from 'ome.'

Griff did a bunny mime with his hand in front of his mouth. 'She don't 'alf give it some. She musta bin vaccinated with a gramophone needle.'

'She'll calm down. "San fairy ann", innit? I mean, she knows it's over.'

'Who you tryin' to convince? Me or you?'

Joey threw the menu down on the table. 'I ain't 'ungry any more.'

'Off yer nosebag?' Griff demanded. 'That's conscience, that is.'

'Will you shut your neck?'

Griff looked past Joey, who had his back to the door. His face altered.

'She's back, Joey!' he said in a tight voice.

Joey froze, not moving a muscle. 'Has she seen me?'

'I think so . . .'

Joey sat rigidly upright while Griff pretended to hide behind him.

'Here she comes,' Griff said.

Joey forced a smile, turned to face Liz. His face sagged. There was no one there! Griff began go roar with laughter, nearly falling off his chair.

'You great prawn,' Joey said.

Griff pointed to Joey's face, which had gone several shades paler. 'Your face!' he shouted with laughter.

Joey grabbed a plastic tomato filled with ketchup from the table, squirted a stream at Griff. Griff moved nimbly to one side and the stream of ketchup landed full on the back of the cabbie sitting behind Griff. He turned slowly, uncomfortably, to see Joey with the plastic tomato still in his hand. Joey tried to put on an apologetic smile as the cabbie, a big man with rolled up sleeves, gave him a look like a wet razor blade.

TWO

THE GYM over the Thomas A'Beckett in the Old Kent Road echoed with the scuffling and squeaking of rubber and leather. There was the curious intensity of extreme physical work in a confined space. Kenny Fox, wearing a headguard, was sparring with a useful young southpaw called Leon Cole. Eddie Chapman was watching every detail with Maxi Lane, an ex-heavyweight champion. Standing well back from the ring so they wouldn't distract Kenny, Billy Fox had brought Andy. The boy watched, wide-eyed, the flurry of action all around him.

Eddie and Maxi shouted advice and strategy as the fighters circled each other between clashes. The sparring was clearly for real, Leon coming in hard to try to pin Kenny on the ropes while Kenny cleverly turned him time and time again. When the sparring round ended the fighters went to their corners, Maxi wiping Leon's face with a towel while Kenny came back to Eddie. Kenny listened, breathing hard, while Eddie talked fast in a low voice.

'He fights just like Charlie Locke, that's why I brought him in. You've got to stay away from him . . . an' Charlie. You can't afford to brawl with Charlie Locke, that's just what he wants. You've got more skill than he's ever seen. Use it, *use* it, Kenny. Charlie's going to be looking for a fight.' Eddie tapped Kenny's head. 'You got to use this. Find a pattern, read him, make him come to you, watch them left crosses. Get that right hand going. He's a southpaw so he's open to right hand counters. Draw his lead and cross.'

At the start of the next round Leon came tearing into Kenny, roughing him up deliberately. Kenny followed instructions, boxing him off, but Leon came after him and it began to get scrappy.

'Ain't it gettin' a bit strong, Eddie?' Maxi was getting concerned.

'Charlie Locke is no sugar plum fairy,' Eddie said, then called to Kenny: 'Draw his lead and cross.'

Suddenly it got really rough. Kenny began to lose control, the two fighters started to slug it out.

'It's gettin' a bit naughty, Eddie!' Maxi shouted.

'Leave it out, you two,' Eddie called out.

But now the two were going at each other like fighting dogs. Maxi and Eddie ducked under the ropes to pull them apart before someone got hurt. Maxi grabbed hold of Leon who was fighting to get at Kenny, while Eddie forced Kenny back towards his corner. Slowly the two boxers calmed down, standing glaring at one another until Maxi led Leon away for a shower. As Kenny leaned against the ropes, Eddie put an arm round his shoulder.

'What happened, Kenny?'

'I dunno; sorry, Eddie.'

'I want to know, Kenny.'

' 'E fancies 'imself.'

'He's a bit tasty,' Eddie said.

' 'E's a plank! Said somethin'.'

'What?'

'Ah . . . just mouth,' Kenny shrugged.

'I want to know.'

'Reckoned 'e could take me any time.'

'That way he could.' Eddie looked hard at Kenny, who looked back in surprise.

'What?'

'If that'd been for money he'd've knocked seven colours of shit out of you. He's a street fighter, an animal. Just like Charlie Locke, only not so fast, not as fit and not as dangerous. Charlie's a bit special, don't forget that. Twenty-three fights, twenty-two wins. Fourteen inside the distance.'

Eddie paused a moment to see his words were sinking in, then went on. 'He's going to come looking for you, son. He'll try the lot. Nut, thumbs, tread on yer feet and he'll give you plenty of verbal. You lose control like you just did, he's going to take you out. You can't afford a war with him, Kenny. You try it and he'll cut you to pieces.'

Billy watched from a distance while Eddie led Kenny off to the changing rooms. He'd been keeping a close eye on Andy and was pleased to see that the boy had taken all the action in his stride. It hadn't frightened him a bit. Now Billy fitted a huge pair of boxing gloves on Andy and knelt on the floor beside him, teaching him the straight left. Andy watched with great concentration as Billy spoke.

'Chin,' Billy pointed. 'In here.' He tucked his chin into his shoulder. 'Now you . . . good, good.'

Andy copied every move as Billy demonstrated a number of punches. When Eddie Chapman walked back into the gym, Billy mimed to Andy that he was going over to talk and that Andy should keep practising.

'Glad you give him a right telling off, Eddie.'

'That's his one real weak point, Billy. That temper of his.'

'Gets it from me.'

'If Kenny keeps cool, uses his noddle, he can outbox any of the hard men.' Eddie shook his head sadly. 'If he don't, it's simple. He's going to get cut and beaten.'

Eddie suddenly noticed little Andy poking out his straight left like a good 'un and had to smile.

'He's beginning to look sharp, Billy. You're training him well.'

'He's going to need it. Nobody's going to take the piss out of 'im when he's older.'

Ray Fox ordered drinks for his brothers Vin and Joey, one for himself and one for Albert, the landlord. They were standing at the end of a long bar, right in the middle of the Fox manor. The pub, a temple of stucco and mahogany, hadn't changed since the days when they delivered the beer on horse-drawn drays. It was a 'local' in the true sense and rarely attracted passing trade. Behind the bar hung framed photographs of Kenny in action in the ring. Albert, a huge man with a beer gut from drinking twenty Worthingtons a day, put the drinks on the bar and gave Ray the change from a fiver.

'Was the booze delivered?' Ray asked Vin.

'Last night,' Vin nodded. 'Dead reasonable too.'

'Told yer. He owed me a favour.' Ray took a fist of notes from his pocket and peeled off fifty quid, holding it out to Vin. 'This should cover my share of the booze and grub.'

'That's too much,' Vin said.

'Take it.' Ray pushed the money into Vin's hand. Vin put it away.

'I'll square up with you later, Vin,' said Joey. As he looked over Vin's shoulder, Joey nudged his brothers. He was the first to spot the Macey brothers, George and Frank, come into the pub. They were a tasty pair, well dressed, in their late thirties. George, the eldest, wore a couple of heavy rings on his punching hand.

'Hey up!' Joey said. ' 'Ere comes Handsome and Gristle!'

Once the two sets of brothers had clocked each other's presence in the pub they acted as if the others didn't exist. But the charade of indifference didn't fool any of the customers, nor Albert who went up to the other end of the bar to serve the Maceys. Vin, Ray and Joey continued their conversation about the party for Billy.

'Had the Joanna tuned,' Vin said.

'Queenie'll love that,' Joey said. Queenie was Billy's younger sister, a good pub pianist, who could always be relied on for some of the old London songs.

'Who you bringin', Joey?' Ray asked.

'No one, can't be bothered.'

Vin and Ray looked at each other. This didn't sound like Joey.

'Don't give me that old gee,' Vin said. 'What about that Suzy?'

'Went an' got married, didn't she? To a red sea pedestrian with a pussy shop.'

'She was a tasty little turn. I could've obliged that,' Ray said.

'Bit skinny,' said Vin.

'Leave off,' Joey sighed.

Vin finished his drink. 'I'm going to slide. Got a lot ter do.'

'Me too,' said Joey.

'Give us a lift.' Ray drank up. 'I left me motor. Walked.'

'I thought you looked knackered,' Joey pulled a face at Ray as he moved away from the bar. 'Cheers, Albert,' he said.

'Give Billy my best,' Albert called.

The Fox brothers moved towards the pub door. Halfway there George Macey turned to his brother, deliberately raising his voice so the whole pub could hear.

'It's the old slag's birthday,' he said.

'Birthday? He wasn't born, someone found 'im under a stone.'

The Fox brothers froze, turned slowly and stared at the Maceys who didn't look up. Ray started to move in but Vin stopped him.

'Leave it, Ray. They're all trap, always were.'

George Macey made a show of clearing an ear with his finger. 'Did I 'ear someone say somethin'?'

Albert tried to intervene. 'You're beggin' for it, son.'

'Hole,' Frank said, pointing to his mouth. 'Shut it, Albert.'

Ray was standing by a table where an old man had been tucking into a thick cheese roll. He leaned over to grab the roll, took out the wedge of cheese and threw it in a swift movement at the Maceys. It hit George on the chest and lodged in his lapel, leaving a greasy butter stain when he moved to let it fall to the ground.

'That's what rats eat,' Ray said.

There was a moment of suspense in the pub, before Frank started to move forward. George quickly put an arm on him to hold him back.

'Sit down.'

The Maceys glared at the Fox brothers, who walked slowly out of the pub door. Ray was the last to leave and George had a last word at his back.

'You've got some comin',' he spat.

Ray turned, gave him a long and hard look. George turned back to the bar as Ray walked out.

Smokers cafe was a regular stop for Billy on the days he spent with Andy. The boy always had a good appetite and Smoker, a bony, tattooed ex-merchant seaman was an old friend. This morning they sat and smoked a couple of Billy's Havanas, watching Andy tuck into a plate of egg and chips. Smoker was telling Billy about a dodge at the tracks where they'd fixed a favourite with rubber bands on the front paws. When the dog came out of the trap, it couldn't spread its front claws to get a grip. By the time the bands broke off the other dogs were halfway home. They'd picked up some good bets, Smoker was saying, when the door opened and Skegg slipped in. A ferret-faced little slag, he had the look of a man who doesn't expect much from life. He sat down quickly at a table by the door, but not before Billy had spotted him.

'What's he doin' here?'

'He comes in sometimes.'

'And you serve him?'

'Got to make a livin', Billy,' Smoker said apologetically.

'He's rubbish.'

'Yeah, well.'

'Ain't you closed, Smoker?' Billy insisted. 'It's gettin' late.'

'Yeah, suppose it is a bit.' Smoker got up and went over to Skegg. 'Sorry, mate. We're closed.'

'Closed?'

'Half day today.'

'I only want a cup of tea and a sandwich,' Skegg said reasonably.

'I turned the urn off. Sorry.'

'What about them?' Skegg pointed to the other people in the cafe.

'They're just finishing.'

Skegg looked across at Billy, suddenly realising what was happening. He stood up slowly.

'Oh, I get it.' He nodded across at Billy. 'King Billy?'

'Look, mate.' Smoker tightened up. 'Why don't you just leave?'

Skegg moved out from his table, turned to Billy. 'You're a nasty old bastard, aren't you?'

Billy took a pull on his cigar, blowing a spiral of smoke at the little man.

'You think you own the bloody manor, don't you?' Skegg walked up to Billy. 'Let me put you straight, Billy Fox. There's a lot of people round 'ere reckon you're an arrogant old pig!'

Billy knotted his fist. 'Listen, grass, if you ain't out of that door in five seconds you'll be walkin' home on your elbows.'

Skegg walked out of the cafe and slammed the door.

Billy pointed to Andy's empty plate. 'Got some ice cream for the boy?' he asked Smoker calmly.

Joey Fox let himself into his flat near Wandsworth Common, took off his leather jacket and flung it on a chair. He stared round. It was always untidy, but today it was really a mess. That bloody parrot, he thought, seeing the big cage empty and starting to look for the bird. Popeye, an African Grey, had been on a field day. Birdshit all over the curtains and furniture, holes pecked in the new lampshade. Joey poked his finger through the holes and spotted Popeye perched up on a curtain rail.

Joey tried to talk the bird down. The horrible fowl just laughed at him until he grabbed the tin case that held his competition snooker cue and poked at the bird. Down the parrot flapped, in a flurry of feathers and hideous squawks. Joey stalked it as it waddled, grumbling, across the floor.

He was just coaxing the bird back into its cage, a thick magazine held like a shield to stop it pecking, when he heard a movement behind him. He quickly closed the door of the cage and turned to see Liz. She was thirty-three and attractive, but with a neurotic face. Joey was startled.

'How did you . . .?'

'I had a set cut.' Liz held up some keys. 'When I borrowed yours.' Liz moved towards Joey as if to kiss him but Joey backed away, moving Popeye's cage as an excuse.

'I kept phoning!' Liz said.

'You know I'm never in.'

'I left messages all over. Didn't you get *any* of them?'

'I told you, Liz, two weeks back.' Joey put an I'm-giving-it-you-straight note in his voice, but this wasn't what Liz wanted to hear. She looked round the flat.

'You can see I haven't been round here recent.'

'Liz, listen to me—' But she was already moving round, tidying up.

'You are a scruffy bugger, Joey.' She picked up his jacket. 'This your *new* jacket?'

'You're not listening!'

Suddenly Liz noticed the mess Popeye had made. 'That filthy bird. You got to get rid of it, Joey. I mean, you're never in enough to look after him properly . . .'

Joey grabbed Liz and shook her. She went very still.

'For Christ's sake, Liz. Remember what we said when it started?'

'No,' Liz said flatly.

'Yes you do. We said when it stopped bein' a giggle . . . that's it, finito. Remember?'

'No.'

'Yes you bloody do!'

'You said you loved me.'

'I said a lot of things . . . yer do, don't yer?' Joey was embarrassed.

'You didn't mean it?'

'Not the way you took it.'

'What way was that, Joey?'

'You know. You got all moody.' He tried to get out of it. 'Anyway, you're married.'

'That never bothered you before.'

'It did. You know it did . . . I said.'

'That first night, you knew I was married.' Liz was getting hysterical. 'You couldn't get back here quick enough. Don't give me all that you're married business. Not now. Not ever!'

Joey gave up. 'There's the door,' he pointed.

Liz pushed her body into Joey's. He tried to back off but she clung to him.

'We don't have to go out,' Liz said desperately. 'I'll come round, just you an' me, Joey. Once a week, that's all. As long as I can see you once a week.'

Liz tried to kiss him but he turned away. 'Please, Joey.' She dropped her hand between his legs. He wrenched away, holding out his hand. 'I'll have them keys,' he said.

'You horrible bastard!' Liz screamed, hurling the keys at Joey's head. They smashed into the parrot's cage as she came at Joey with her nails. Joey grabbed her wrists, threw her across a chair. Her shoulder bag burst open, spilling its contents over the floor. Liz caught hold of a plastic styling comb and as Joey came forward stabbed it hard into his shoulder. There was a moment of total stillness when Liz realised what she'd done. Blood oozed through Joey's shirt. Liz dropped the comb, put a fist to her mouth as if to stop herself being sick. She turned and ran out of the flat.

THREE

ANNA'S car pulled up outside a Victorian mansion block near Sloane Square. Anna led the way up to the first floor flat. Phil looked round, impressed. Antique and modern furniture well mixed, oriental carpets, good paintings, a baby grand tucked away in a corner. The whole place screamed money and good taste.

'This is *yours*?'

'An aunt left it to me.' To Anna it was just a flat. 'You hungry?'

'I don't eat a lot.' Phil was a little ill at ease.

'There's a drink over there if you want it.' She pointed to a lacquered Chinese drinks cabinet.

'Rather have a cup of tea.'

Phil looked at the wall full of books while Anna went into the kitchen. He fingered through the titles for a minute or two, then followed her out. Anna laid the scrubbed pine table while the kettle boiled and began putting out bread and cheese. Phil had told her about Billy's party in the car. He suddenly had a thought.

'Why don't you come with me?'

'I'd love to, I really would . . . I've got to meet my parents. They're up from the country, there's no way I can duck it.'

'Just a thought,' Phil said. He was surprised to find he felt disappointed.

'A *nice* thought. Will you come and see me tomorrow instead?'

'What about your feller?'

'He's in Yorkshire,' Anna shrugged.

Vin was at his desk going through some paperwork when Clem came in. It was late afternoon. Clem had a swelling over one eye and a bruise on his neck. He was carrying the stolen Kango and box of chisels.

'Jesus, Clem, what the 'ell 'ave you been up to?'

'Sorry, guvnor.' Clem didn't sound sorry. 'We 'ad to go down there! That little shit 'ead put the poison in. One of the labourers 'ad it!'

Clem dumped the Kango and chisels on Vin's desk.

*

Nan let herself into Billy Fox's house with a key Connie had given her. She was looking forward to this evening and had her party clothes in a small suitcase. She called out from the hallway, but there was no reply. Nan moved up the stairs, called again.

'Kenny?'

'Up here,' Kenny called back.

Nan stopped outside the bathroom, tried the door which was locked.

'I'm in the bath,' Kenny shouted.

'Unlock the door.'

'You rude lady.'

'I'll scrub your back,' Nan giggled.

'I'll tell my mum of you!'

Nan smiled. 'You wait till you see my new dress. Very sexy!' She moved away into Kenny's room. It was very ordered, his suit laid out, shoes polished, shirt hanging on the wardrobe with cufflinks in place. Nan put her case on the bed, carefully took out her party dress and laid it out. She started to undress. When she was wearing only her panties, she suddenly realised that Kenny was standing behind her, wearing his bathrobe.

'I can see through it,' Kenny said in a serious voice.

'What?'

'Your new frock.'

'You silly . . .' Nan giggled as Kenny closed in. 'I'm late already, Kenny.'

He put his arms around her but she slipped away.

'No, Kenny.'

Kenny lifted his robe to show his legs. 'How do they look?'

'Have you been drinking?' Nan laughed.

'They say it weakens the legs.'

'You what?'

'Sex!' Kenny dived and wrestled her, screaming and laughing, on to the bed.

The party had started at Vin's house. Vin was ushering in the first guests, his three kids rushing round excitedly. Billy, dressed to the nines with a rose in his button-hole, was smoking a Havana and holding court. Griff was looking after the bar. Ray arrived with his girl, Carol, very sexy in a low-cut dress, each carrying a monster-size bottle of bubbly. They handed them over to Griff, who pretended he couldn't hold the two bottles and staggered off under the weight to put them in ice buckets. They greeted Billy. Ray took a small, wrapped present from his inside pocket. Billy opened it and held up a beautiful antique gold pocket watch. When everyone had ooh'd and aah'd their appreciation, Ray showed his father how to press a little catch on one side. The watch opened to delicate chimes, bringing applause from the circle of friends. The front doorbell rang and Vin let in another batch of guests, closely followed by Phil.

'We was expectin' you earlier,' Vin said. There had always been a sharpness between them.

'I got a lift a bit later.'

Vin looked at Phil's student gear. 'Ain't you going to change?'

'What for?'

'Look decent, put a suit on.'

'I haven't got a suit,' Phil said truthfully.

'What's all this then?' Vin fingered Phil's shoulder-length hair. 'Contemplatin' a sex change?'

'Don't start, Vin,' Phil said earnestly.

'Well,' Vin shrugged, 'if you want to look like a bleedin' pikey!'

Phil moved past him into the party room and was immediately spotted by Connie, who rushed over and hugged him.

'You got to watch what you say now,' Billy said proudly to the room in general. He indicated Phil. 'He's writin' a book about us all!'

'Happy birthday, Pop,' said Phil, handing over a package.

'Ta son. Well, what've we got 'ere?' He opened the present, his eyes lighting up as he saw the LPs. 'George Lewis. The King of New Orleans!' It was his favourite music, as everyone knew.

Someone had just put on the George Lewis when Kenny and Nan, both looking very smart, came in with Eddie, Kenny's manager.

' 'Ere 'e is, ladies and gentlemen,' Billy called. 'The next welterweight champion of Great Britain.' Billy raised Kenny's arm like a referee. Kenny lowered his arm and raised Billy's instead.

'And here *he* is, ladies and gentlemen. The heavyweight champion of the Fox family!'

There was a general cheer for Billy, who was smiling from ear to ear.

'You're looking a picture, Nan love.' Billy appealed to the others. 'Don't she look lovely?' He turned back to Nan. 'When are you two going to do an altar job?'

'When he asks me!'

Kenny took a small, beautifully wrapped present from his pocket.

'Happy birthday, Pop. This is from me and Nan.'

'Don't change the subject. When are you going to marry this lovely girl?'

'How about September?' Kenny asked casually.

'Do you mean it?' Nan asked him quickly.

'It ain't somethin' you joke about.'

Nan jumped with delight to give Kenny a big kiss while Billy, beaming, opened his present. It was a pair of cufflinks made like tiny boxing gloves.

'Nan's dad got them specially made for us.'

'They're 'andsome! Help me put them in, Con.'

The doorbell rang again.

'I'm in and out like a poacher's dog,' Vin said as he went to answer it.

He couldn't believe what he saw. His jaw sagged, he stood amazed as if seeing a vision. Joey was standing in the doorway in immaculate drag, beautifully made up in a real Danny La Rue special.

'Jesus, Joey!'

'The name's Pearl, big boy.' Joey hit Vin over the head with a handbag as he minced in. 'Announce me.'

Vin, trying hard to keep a straight face, walked into the party. 'Billy!' he called across the crowded room. 'Someone for you.'

Then Joey/Pearl slunk in, doing his Mae West.

'Which one of you handsome hunks is Billy Fox?' he drawled.

'That's me, darlin'!' Billy loved anything like this and couldn't wait to join in. 'What can I do fer you?'

'It ain't what you can do for *me*!' Joey pressed up against Billy. The guests were falling about laughing.

'Those sporting gentlement in the Crown took up a collection,' Joey went on. 'I'm your birthday present. The name's Pearl. Light the blue touch paper and stand well clear!'

Billy reached out, grabbed Joey and they started to jive to the George Lewis band, still playing on the gramophone. The guests cleared a space in the centre of the room, clapping them on. As Billy spun Joey round faster and faster the false boobs slipped. Billy tried to help as Joey made a gag out of getting them back in place and they carried on their crazy dance, twisting and twirling in the middle of the party. Finally the music ran out and Joey dug into his handbag to find Billy's present. Everyone gathered round as Billy unwrapped it. He looked puzzled and held it up for inspection. It was beautifully knitted, a long thin stocking with a little drawstring at the end.

'Gawd knows what it is,' Billy laughed.

'It's a Willy Warmer . . . for them long winter nights.' Joey placed it in the appropriate position to demonstrate. Everyone roared with laughter.

'Going to put it on, Billy?' Renie asked wickedly.

'Right!' Billy responded immediately to the challenge, unzipping his fly.

'Billy Fox, don't you dare!' Connie said laughing.

Billy zipped up, then he held out the Willy Warmer, stretching its already considerable length.

'Strewth!'

'Send it to George Macey. He's a big prick,' Ray suggested to a roar of appreciation.

Joey slipped upstairs to change into a suit and recover his breath from the dancing. He was just massaging his shoulder to ease the wound Liz had made with the comb that afternoon, when Phil passed by and saw him through the partly open door.

'You okay, Joey?' Phil sensed something wrong.

'Never better, my old intellectual.' Joey forced a smile.

Downstairs the party was in full swing. A big group gathered round the piano where Queenie started to play, joining in the songs. Queenie was just soloing on:

'Last week down our alley came a toff,
Nice old geezer with a nasty cough,
Sees my missus, takes 'is topper off
In a very gentlemanly way.'

Everyone was waiting for the chorus:

'Wot cher! all the neighbours cried,
Who're yer goin' to meet, Bill?
'Ave yer bought the street, Bill?
Laugh! I thought I should 'ave died,
Knocked 'em in the Old Kent Road!'

*

In the street outside, the party sounded like a right old Cockney ding dong. A large, black motor approached and stopped in the shadows as if to listen to the music, laughter and applause coming from the house. Inside were the Maceys and two other heavy faces. They slipped out of the car. George opened the boot to take out a sack. The Macey brothers moved silently past the cars parked in front of the house, into the pitch black garden and round to the back wall by the kitchen. Renie was washing some glasses. When she finished she put the clean glasses on a tray and walked out, switching off the light. George Macey opened the back door very carefully. Frank Macey moved a few yards into the kitchen with the sack and opened it close to the floor. A dozen rats scuttled into the kitchen and started to move through the house.

In the party room there were calls for more songs and Queenie started an intro.

'Come on, Billy. "Father's Grave",' Queenie called. Billy sang lustily.

'Oh, they're moving Father's grave to build a sewer,
They're moving it regardless of expense.
They're shifting his remains to put in five-inch drains,
To irrigate some posh bloke's residence.'

Everyone was round the piano now. Joey moved up alongside a young bird he'd had an eye on, and they all joined with Billy in a reprise of his verse.

Suddenly Joey's young bird stiffened as she saw two rats at her feet. She jumped and then screamed at the top of her lungs. There was total chaos as the men started to chase the rats out and the women kept trying to get out of the way. Joey's bird scrambled right up on top of the piano.

Outside, the Maceys had been waiting for the commotion to start, and they roared with laughter.

'Happy birthday, Billy,' said George Macey, as he dropped the big car into gear and accelerated away.

Later that evening, after the rats had been dealt with and the party had come back into some kind of order, Griff opened the two giant bottles of champagne and everyone had a full glass. The door burst open and Vin wheeled in a huge birthday cake, with seventy burning candles, on an old Covent Garden porter's barrow. The immediate family gathered round Billy at the barrow. He was very moved, almost in tears, as he slapped the handles of the barrow.

'I thought I'd seen the last of one of these,' he said. 'Forty years workin' in the Garden, you see a few things. Mark you, that was when Covent Garden was a real place with real people. Not like it is now, a seventy-acre public lavatory.' There was laughter all around him.

'I well remember the man who give me my first job in the Garden. Mr Matthews. I never knew his other name, he was always *Mister* Matthews. An' he was quite a philosopher. I remember he once said a man can think himself very fortunate if he can name three *real friends*.'

Billy gestured round the room. 'Well, that means I'm a very fortunate feller, because I've got a house full.'

He put an arm round Connie.

'More than that, I've got a lovely wife and five sons any man would be proud of . . . I always wanted a daughter but out kept poppin' these little bastards!'

There was more laughter.

'Seventy seems a lot of years but really it's nothin'. We're on this earth for a very short while, so why not enjoy it? I have, I know that. Every second of every one of them seventy years. If I had it all again I wouldn't change a thing . . . 'cept perhaps old Ruby goin' so early. But then I wouldn't 'ave had the pleasure of Connie's company for the past thirty years.' He paused and looked round his audience cheerfully. 'Anyway, you haven't come here to hear speeches, the night's still young, the booze seems to be holding out, the rats are gone . . . and these candles are gettin' bloody 'ot.'

Billy raised his glass.

'I drink a toast. To my darling wife, my five boys . . . and my good friends. God bless you all.' He drank down his glass of champagne. 'Now I suppose I've got to blow these buggers out.' Billy looked from the candles to Vin's kids. 'Come on you lot, you've got to help Grandad!'

Billy and the kids blew out the seventy candles to cheers from the crowded room. The circle round Billy broke up as the music started playing. Everyone formed groups to dance the Cokey Cokey and then the Conga, Billy leading the human snake all over the house, up the stairs and through the bedrooms.

While they were upstairs the doorbell rang. Vin had been taking a breather and came out to answer it with a glass in one hand and one of Billy's cigars in the other. It was a woman he'd never seen before, about thirty with dyed hair, not bad looking in a sloppy sort of way.

'Not complaining about the noise, are you?' Vin asked pleasantly.

'No . . . er, no. Could I speak to Joey, Joey Fox?'

'Come in.'

'I'd rather not. I'll wait in my van, it's just across the street.'

'Is there anything wrong, love? I mean, I'm one of his brothers.'

'It won't take a minute. Please tell Joey it's Pat. My name's Pat. He'll understand.'

Vin shut the door. He had a good idea where Joey was. He walked upstairs to the bathroom and knocked. Inside, Joey was with the young bird. He raised a finger to his lips when they heard Vin call Joey's name. Joey pulled a face like a naughty boy and the girl giggled.

'Joey, can I see you?' Vin wasn't giving up. 'It's important, someone to see you – called Pat.'

Joey sobered up immediately – it was Liz's sister.

'Don't go away,' he whispered to the girl and unlocked the door.

Joey walked up to the van. All he could see of Pat was a silhouette and the glow of a cigarette. Joey got in.

'What happened this afternoon?'

'What did she say happened?' There was no reply. 'She bloody stabbed me, that's what happened! Is she all right?' Joey sounded concerned.

'Another half-hour and she would've been shot of this lousy life!'

'What the hell are you on about?'

'Took an overdose, didn't she? They're pumping her out in St Stephen's. She meant it, Joey. This wasn't no cry for help. She bloody meant it!'

*

Back at the party everyone was dancing to soft, slow music, the mood very mellow by now. Joey came back with Vin. He forced a party smile and crossed the room to Connie.

'Fancy a twirl, darlin'?' Joey drew his mother on to the floor and they started to dance. Connie sensed something at once.

'What's wrong, Joey?'

'Wrong? What could be wrong when I'm dancin' with the most beautiful lady here tonight?'

But in the half-light the party mask cracked. Joey's face filled with confusion and guilt.

FOUR

HER face the colour of a cheap envelope, Liz walked slowly out of the main entrance of the hospital. She wore no make-up and her clothes looked as if they'd been thrown on. As she moved towards the main gate an ambulance had to brake hard to avoid hitting her. She leaned against a wall, her vision blurred. She felt weak and disoriented. A nurse just about to go on duty came up but her concerned face seemed distorted. Liz couldn't make out what she was saying. Only odd words came through.

'Are you . . . come from . . . suppose . . . out here . . . better inside.'

Liz forced herself away from the wall and heard herself speak from what seemed a great distance.

'Bit dizzy . . . gone now. All right, thanks.'

Liz moved on towards the main gate. The nurse watched her through it, then turned to walk briskly into the hospital. Liz walked slowly, determined to put as much distance between the hospital and herself as possible. A taxi clattered outside the main gate as she turned into the street. Reacting against it, Liz covered her face with her hands. When she looked up, she realised her behaviour was attracting the attention of a queue of people waiting at a bus stop. She ignored them and walked on down the street.

Vin and Renie were clearing up after the party. The room was a wreck with dirty glasses, plates and cutlery everywhere. Ashtrays overflowed with cigarette and cigar butts, the wrapping paper from Billy's presents was heaped in the fireplace.

'Saw Joey with her once, I think,' Vin said, checking the bottles to see how much booze was left.

'Did you know she was married?' Renie was emptying ashtrays into a metal bin.

'Maybe it wasn't her,' Vin was evasive.

'Joey never said nothing?'

'You know Joey. If he don't *want* yer to know . . . She didn't *look* married.'

'How long's it been going on?'

'Griff reckons six months.'

'What did Griff say?'

'Not a lot.'

'Vin!' Renie knew she wasn't getting the whole story.

'He wasn't exactly sober. None of us was . . . said she was a bit neurotic.'

'Oh, of course,' Renie said sarcastically. 'I suppose it's all *her* fault.'

'I didn't say . . .'

'It don't sound like Joey comes out of this too good. I sometimes wonder about Joey. He's like a great soft kid, never grown up.'

'Maybe that's what turns them on,' Vin said tartly. He could feel an argument brewing and wanted to stop it, but Renie wasn't having any.

'Joey hurts people, Vinnie. He doesn't mean to do it, but he hurts people. What about Billy? Does Billy know?'

'We didn't want to muck up the party. It was goin' down a treat.'

'Someone'll have to tell him.'

'Joey 'ad a word with Connie,' Vin admitted reluctantly.

'He'll go spare!' Renie said.

The front doorbell was ringing. Joey stumbled out of his bedroom, face like a squeezed toothpaste tube. He aimed himself at the door and opened it. Billy was standing there, spruce as ever. Joey took one look at Billy's face and knew what the visit was about, but he couldn't help wondering to himself how the old man did it. He couldn't have had more than five hours sleep, *and* after a very boozy party. Billy walked past Joey into the flat, looking at the disorder disgustedly and sniffing the foetid atmosphere.

'Place stinks,' he said, as he went to a window and threw it open.

'I didn't want to spoil your party,' Joey pleaded.

'That was thoughtful,' Billy said hollowly.

'You know what I mean . . . she's all right, I phoned the hospital.'

'She's all right?' Billy's voice was strange.

'Yeah . . .'

'Belly full of pills, stomach pump. All the indignities. She's in hospital feelin' like death an' here you are rottin' in yer feather!'

Joey pulled a long-suffering face and went to turn away but Billy cuffed him on the ear, knocking him into a chair.

'You just can't keep your shirt over it, can you?' Billy stood over him angrily.

'Hold up, Pop!'

'Ain't there enough little sweeties around?'

'You don't understand.'

'What's there to understand? You've 'ad your feet under some poor bastard's table and that ain't right, Joey. You know that.' Billy waited a moment. 'You goin' to bunny your way out of this one? Who is he? Her old man?'

'Works away. He's never home,' Joey said.

'How very convenient. What's 'is name?'

'Ronnie.'

'Her *married* name,' Billy said impatiently.

'Boyd.'

'Local?'

'You'd 'ave heard if she was.'

'What you goin' to do about it, Joey?'

'What *can* I do?' Joey was a bit lost.

'First off you go to see her. Take her some flowers. Be nice to her, talk to her.'

'She don't listen, Pop. I've been tryin' to put her down gentle for over a month. She keeps ringin' . . . on and bloody on. That's why this place is like it is. I stay out, kipped in the cab a couple of nights.' Joey stared at his father. 'Okay, when I pulled it I knew it was married. But there weren't no crossed legs. I mean, she's bin around. I ain't the first, that's a million.'

'Joey . . . Joey!' Billy shook his head. 'You ain't a kid no more. It ain't no good turnin' round sayin' that, blamin' her. You start messin' with married women an' you're bang in trouble! Why didn' you say something? To me . . . Connie. Vin . . . anyone?'

'I told Griff.'

'Griff's not family.'

'It was my problem,' Joey said stubbornly.

'You know better than that.'

Joey, seeking sympathy, rolled up his shirt to show his wound. 'She bloody stabbed me!'

'Stabbing, suicide.' Billy was shocked. 'Why did yer let it get this far, Joey? Why didn't you come to me, quietly? We could've worked somethin' out. None of this bloody mess need have happened.'

There was a sudden noise from the bedroom.

'What's that?' Billy asked.

'Nothin' ' Joey answered nervously.

'I heard somethin'.'

'Downstairs cat gets in sometimes.'

Billy moved towards the bedroom. Joey quickly slipped between Billy and the bedroom door.

'It's nothin' Pop!'

Billy pushed Joey out of the way, threw open the bedroom door. The young bird from the party was getting dressed as quietly as she could. Billy stood in the doorway glaring at her. She looked startled and smiled nervously.

'Sorry, Joey. I . . . I dropped me shoe.'

Billy closed the door and turned to Joey with a look of pained sadness.

'You wicked little bastard,' he said.

Ray cruised the Jaguar across Battersea Bridge. He was giving Phil a lift up to town on his way into the club.

'Where d'yer want me to drop you?'

'Anywhere near Sloane Square.'

'They love a bit of rough,' Ray smiled knowingly.

'You're talking from experience, of course?'

'Not many! I had this little blonde turn 'bout two years back. Daddy was a top brief, divorced. She lived with 'im in a big 'ouse in Holland Park.' Ray smiled at the recollection. 'She was a right 'andful.'

'What happened?'

'She come on strong one night an' I give her a smack. She loved it. Kinky for it, she was.' He pulled a face.

'She ended up with some South African who was into all that. Mark you, 'e did have a couple of million to go with it!' Ray paused. 'Why don't you bring 'er down the club?'

'I only met her yesterday.'

'I'd behave meself,' Ray exaggerated. '*Talk proper* like.'

'Leave off, Ray.'

'Well . . . yer know, first impressions.'

Ray pulled up in Sloane Square. He leaned across for a parting word with Phil through the open window.

'Make sure she's not married,' he joked.

'Poor old Joey.'

'I bet Billy's given him a right coating! Maybe see you later, eh?'

Ray laughed as he drove off. Phil crossed Sloane Square, making his way to Anna's flat.

Phil rang Anna's doorbell. After a few moments the door was opened by an expensively dressed woman in her forties.

'Is . . . er, is Anna in?' Phil managed to ask.

The woman looked him over. 'No. Was she expecting you?'

'We didn't say a time.'

'Anna didn't mention she was expecting anyone.'

'Will she be very long?'

'I'm sorry, I have no idea.'

'We were going out,' Phil explained.

The woman suddenly seemed to make up her mind, standing to one side as though to invite him in.

'I'm Anna's mother.'

In the sitting room a pot of freshly percolated coffee stood on a tray. Anna's mother sat down and poured herself a cup but didn't offer Phil any.

'I thought I knew most of Anna's friends in London,' she said.

Phil made a point of being polite. 'I'm at the university.'

'Forgive me, but you seem rather old for an undergraduate.'

'Mature student. Moral Philosophy.'

'Do you know Anthony?' she asked suddenly.

'Anthony? Anna's feller?'

'They're nearly engaged,' Anna's mother said formidably.

There was a long silence, broken by the sound of the front door opening and Anna's appearance in the doorway. Her face lit up as she saw Phil.

Her mother watched her enthusiasm with concern.

'I offered Philip some coffee but he didn't want any,' Anna's mother lied. Phil was amazed and looked at her. She returned his look, as if challenging him.

Later, walking down the King's Road, Phil and Anna threaded their way through the Sunday tourists and window shoppers. Anna had noticed her mother's attitude. She tried to draw Phil on the subject, but he didn't want to make any comment. Anna sighed.

'She's not always like that. She's going through a difficult time. My father is older, quite a bit older. It's funny, I never think of him ever having been young. He married before . . . She died.'

They were nearly at World's End. They walked into a little coffee shop and sat down at a corner table.

'I have a step-brother, Michael. He's one of those people who has an opinion about everything. He talks a lot but never listens.'

'Your mother said you're "nearly engaged"?'

'Poor Anthony,' Anna smiled.

'You make him sound like a victim.'

'Anthony is a victim by vocation. We have what you might call an eroding relationship. My parents made sure of that.'

'They don't approve?'

'Much more subtle than that . . . they make a show of their approval.'

Liz wandered the streets. She stopped at the kerb and looked up the road at the oncoming traffic. She closed her eyes tight and deliberately stepped out. There was a scream of tyres and a hiss of air brakes. A huge lorry screeched to a stop only two feet away.

Ray Fox mixed himself a Bloody Mary behind the bar of his club. When he turned he saw that Terry, a local burglar who specialised in big houses, had slipped in quietly. Terry looked worried.

'You look like you could use a drop of medicine,' said Ray, pouring him a large scotch. 'What's up?'

'I'm poncing a favour, Ray. If I can't sort somethin' out, I'm goin' to be up on one.'

'You bin workin'?'

'Yeah . . . an' I dropped a bollock. They was round this morning to give me a little tug. Lucky I was out. My Jeannie got word to me.'

'What they got on you?'

'Christ knows . . . I thought it'd gone off sweet as a nut. Good little earner.'

'Maybe they were just bein' busy. Goin' for a pull on yer form?'

'Na . . . Jeannie said they were tryin'.'

'Anyone we know?'

Terry shrugged. 'A DS called Hough?'

Ray shook his head slowly. He'd never heard of him.

'Said he was a pushy bleeder.'

'Ain't they all?'

'I can't work it out, Ray.'

'This bit of work. Someone offered it up?'

'Bob Leonardi.'

Ray nodded. 'He's reliable.'

'I give him a twoer, he was well pleased.' Terry thought for a moment. 'I always work solo, dead careful. Christ, I was in and out in eleven minutes!'

'Maybe someone saw yer?'

'Too dark.'

'Did they do the house?'

'No. Wish they 'ad. They'd still be lookin'.' Terry downed his glass and Ray turned back to the optics to fill it.

'But they 'ad a warrant?'

'Yeah . . . why?'

'Bit smelly.' Ray handed Terry the scotch. 'They must of known you'd already knocked it out. Who did yer place it with . . . Lakey?'

'Yeah. If that little dog's gone the other way, he's goin' to get hurt!'

'What's the favour?'

'I was 'ere, wan' I? That night?'

'What night was that then?'

'Week las' Thursday.'

Ray considered. He wouldn't do this for anyone, but he and Terry went way back. He smiled.

'Got a feelin' you was, now I come to think of it.'

'I wouldn't lumber you, Ray, but Jeannie, bless 'er 'eart, couldn't think of anythink else on the spot.'

'You'd better get lost.'

'I'll give you a tinkle, later on like.' Terry finished his drink and turned to leave.

'Don't fret. We'll have it sorted, one way or the other,' Ray said.

'You're a diamond . . . there's a nice little drink in it for yer.' Terry slipped quickly and quietly out of the club. Ray picked up his glass, still half full of Bloody Mary, and topped it up with vodka.

*

Joey was having no luck at the hospital. He got there with a large bunch of flowers, only to be told that Liz wasn't there. The ward sister told him Liz had signed herself out early that morning, saying she was going to her sister's place. The ward sister seemed to think he was Liz's husband and Joey didn't disabuse her. On his way out he passed an old lady who had been left outside the X-ray department, looking like an old dog tied to a railing and abandoned. Joey stopped, turned back, placed the expensive bunch of flowers gently in her lap. Then he moved quickly up the corridor.

Ray was at the piano playing 'As Time Goes By' with one finger when Detective Sergeant Hough came into the club. Ray had him spotted but played it very casual.

'You're late,' he said.

Hough, a big man in his early thirties, snappily dressed, was thrown for a moment. Ray looked at his watch.

'I said twelve. It's goin' on two.'

Hough took out his identification, held it under Ray's nose. Ray went on with his performance.

'Sorry, guv. I was expectin' a piano player.'

'Nice place.' Hough looked around.

'It's a livin'. You workin' or sightseeing?'

Hough put away his ID. 'Get a few faces in, do you?' he asked.

'One or two, now and then.'

'What about Terry Connell?'

'Yeah, he likes a quiet drink.'

'When did you see him last?'

'Terry?' Ray made a show of thinking.

'Recent?' Hough followed up.

'No, not recent.' Ray shook his head and Hough looked eager. ' 'Bout a week back.'

Hough prickled. 'I call that recent.'

'I thought you meant last night. I wasn't in last night, my old man . . .'

'You tryin' to be smart?' Hough interrupted.

'I'm tryin' to be helpful. Want a drink?'

'No.'

Ray got up from behind the piano, walked behind the bar. He took a clean glass and poured himself a vodka. Hough followed him across, sat at the bar. Ray pretended to work it out.

'Friday, Sat'day, Sunday . . . Thursday, must've bin Thursday. Last Thursday.'

Hough stiffened. 'Last Thursday night Terry Connell was doing a climb on a house in Hampstead . . . did you hear me?'

'You sure you don't want a drink?'

'He's marked your card.' Hough watched as Ray sipped his drink. 'Or his missus.'

'Jeannie? I haven't seen her in months.' Ray laughed. 'I couldn't even tell you what colour her hair is now.'

'You're a bastard liar. You know what I mean.'

'I don't and that's a fact,' Ray said calmly.

'He's in the frame.'

'All I can say is, whoever stuck him up is pullin' your chain. I'd 'ave a little talk to the dirty slag.'

'I'm goin' to nick Connell, an' I'm goin' to give him some!'

Ray raised his glass. 'Cheers.'

Hough slapped the glass out of Ray's hand. It flew across the bar and smashed against a wall.

'They told me you was a bit of a tearass,' said the DS.

Ray gripped the bar to hold himself in control. He turned away, picked up another glass and held it to the vodka optic. Hough slipped off the stool and moved away.

'You're just another mouth,' said Hough, and walked out of the bar. Ray smiled, gave him the finger and finished his drink.

FIVE

IT was early afternoon when Phil and Anna walked through South Kensington. As they passed a pub two Hooray Henrys staggered out semi-legless. They were in their late twenties, well dressed but out of condition. Indulgence and a sedentary life had spread their stomachs over their waistbands. They were drunkenly delighted to see Anna.

'Anna! It's little Anna,' one of them shouted.

Anna didn't really want to know but before she could back off and escape he'd thrown a limp arm around her shoulder. 'Anna, darling . . .'

'Hello, Simon,' Anna said unenthusiastically. She looked at the other one. 'I thought you were in Brazil?'

'Argentina, darling,' Simon's friend drawled.

Anna tried to introduce Phil. 'Phil, this is—' But they weren't interested in Phil. Simon slipped his flabby arms round Anna and pulled her close. Anna glanced, embarrassed, at Phil and moved away from Simon.

'We're rather late,' she said.

Simon grabbed her wrist. 'Come and have a drink,' he insisted.

Phil had been holding back but now he tried to be tactful.

'I think you've had a skinful, pal,' he said quietly.

'I'm talking to Anna, *pal*!' Simon answered aggressively.

Anna tried to pull away but he held on to her. 'You used to be a friendly little thing,' he insinuated.

Phil moved in, took hold of Simon's wrist and forcibly levered it away. Simon's face flushed with anger. He reached out for Anna again.

'I told you, you're embarrassing her!' Phil flared. In a single violent movement he grabbed the front of Simon's trousers and ripped the waistband and the flies open. Simon was left staggering around on the pavement, trying to hold up his trousers.

'Do you like being embarrassed?'

'You bastard!' Simon's friend shouted and swung at Phil who easily avoided the punch, shooting out a hand to grab his tie.

'Don't start something you can't finish!' Phil remonstrated. Phil dragged the bloke across the pavement, nearly choking him, and knotted his tie round some railings. Anna watched with delight. Simon, trying to hold his trousers together, jumped on Phil's back. Phil swivelled and threw him down on his hands and knees, then kicked him up the arse. Simon fell flat on his face and Phil stood over him, a foot on his ample backside.

'You stay down there until we're gone or you're going to get more than a hangover,' Phil said.

Anna came up, slipped her arm through Phil's and they walked away down the street. Simon wobbled to his feet and started to help his friend untie himself from the railings.

Pat opened the door of her council flat to Joey. She looked as if she hadn't slept all night.

'What do *you* want?'

'To talk to Liz.'

Pat was alarmed. 'She's left the hospital?'

'Early. She signed herself out. She told the sister she was coming to you.'

'She's not here. The silly cow!' Pat bent down to scoop up a young kid crawling along the hall floor. 'Have you been round her place?'

'I come straight here,' Joey said. 'She'd 'ave rung, wouldn't she, if she was at home?'

'Our phone's been cut off. I'll use next door's, she might be there.' She pushed the snotty-faced kid into Joey's arms. 'Hang on to him.'

Pat pushed past him to go to the flat next door and ring the bell. The door was opened by a pregnant black woman.

'Josie, can I use your phone?'

'Help yourself,' Josie said.

Pat went in, followed by Joey with the kid in his arms. Josie gave him a look and reached for the child.

'I'll take him.'

Pat was already dialling. Joey took a ten pence piece from his pocket and offered it to Josie to pay for the call.

'That's too much.'

'Take it.'

Josie took the money. Pat waited while Liz's number rang. She muttered to herself.

'Be there Liz . . . please be there.'

There was no reply. Pat held out the receiver so Joey could hear it ringing.

'You've got to find her, Joey.'

At King's Cross Station the train from Scotland had just arrived. Ronnie Boyd got off, carrying a battered case. Well over six feet tall and powerfully built with a sullen, angular face, he made his way swiftly through the station concourse to a cab rank. There was a sticker showing a North Sea oil rig on the side of his case and his huge knuckles were clenched whitely on the handle.

Alan Haywood stood in the middle of Ray's club looking lost. He was tall with round shoulders, and his pale face looked like he'd been living a life of quiet desperation. Ray suddenly appeared from his upstairs office.

'You made it then,' Ray said.

Haywood nervously ran his tongue across his lips, an unconscious habit.

'Yeah,' he said in a wispy voice.

'Ray Fox,' Ray offered his hand. 'I'm a fan of yours. Used to listen to you a lot at Ronnie's.'

'My pink period.' Haywood pulled down the bottom of one eye to show the white and smiled ruefully.

Ray walked behind the bar, poured himself a glass of good brandy, and watched Haywood's face closely.

'If I give you this gig you're goin' to smell a lot of booze.' He sipped the brandy. 'Think you can handle that?'

'I can try,' Haywood said honestly, and Ray liked him for that.

'How long have you been dry?'

'Eighteen weeks and four days.'

Ray had to smile at the exactness of the reply.

'I'd want you 'ere at nine, on the dot. Through to three.'

'Sounds fair.'

'Where you livin' now?'

'Tooting.'

'You don't drive?'

'They've got my licence framed in the black museum,' Haywood joked.

Ray nodded. 'You make your own way 'ere . . . you get a mini-cab back, on the house.'

'Nice one,' Haywood said appreciatively.

'I'll start you off at a pony a night, see how we go. There's a meal if you want it . . . the first night you turn up pissed, you're out.'

'You're on.'

'Can you start tonight?'

'Don't you want me to audition?' Haywood pointed to the piano.

Ray shook his head. 'If you're half as good as you was, you're still twice as good as anyone else.'

Haywood went over to the piano, lifted the lid and sat hunched over the keyboard staring at it.

'It's a good axe,' Ray told him. 'Should be, I paid a lot of dough for it.'

Haywood ran his fingers over the keys, started to play an old Erroll Garner number, 'Love Is the Strangest Game'. He was *very* good. He turned to Ray, still playing.

' "Arched fingers for Bach, flat fingers for love," ' he quoted.

'Art Tatum,' Ray said.

'You know your jazz.'

'I was raised on it. My old man's a connoisseur.'

Ray sipped his brandy and let the music pour over him like warm rain.

It was a fine afternoon in the park at Crystal Palace. Billy Fox walked alongside his old mate Charlie Shepherd. They moved round the edge of the sports stadium. In the distance a runner plodded stubbornly along the tarmac track. When the preliminaries were over, Billy turned to the business in hand. Charlie was a local bookmaker and had the reputation, like Billy, of knowing everyone in his manor and most of what was going on. He was known to all his friends as Chuck.

'Tell me about Ronnie Boyd, Chuck.'

'What do you want to know for?'

Billy ignored the question. 'Is he a villain?'

'No, but he's a handful. I've seen him on the malice. He took on five spades in a drinker in Streatham . . . he done three of 'em, the other two turned white!'

'He sounds useful,' Billy said with considerable understatement.

'He ain't around much,' Chuck said. 'Works the rigs. He's a diver, underwater welder. What's the bother, Billy?'

'No bother.'

'Yet?' Chuck completed the sentence.

'What's his missus like?'

'Don't know much about her.' Chuck thought for a minute. 'Younger than he is. A looker, if you like the sort. Word is she puts it about a bit when he's away. This got anythink to do with your Joey?'

Billy wasn't giving anything away. 'What makes you ask that?'

'Well, you know Joey . . . get his leg across anythink that moves. Seen him round here a couple of times, recent like. I thought to meself, he's well out of his manor.'

Chuck looked Billy between the eyes. 'If he's been givin' her one and Ronnie's found out, I'd get him insured!'

Liz was still wandering the streets aimlessly. She looked in a shop window at a spring display of wedding clothes. A group of mannequins represented a bride and bridesmaids. Liz stared at the virgin white silk of the bride's dress. To her horror a small stain of blood appeared on the breast spreading out until the front of the dress was scarlet. Liz quickly turned her head away from the window, her eyes tightly shut.

Pat's council flat was a mess, the kid was bawling somewhere and she felt awful. When the doorbell rang she dragged herself to answer it, feeling at least a hundred years old. She opened the door and her stomach knotted.

'Ronnie!'

He pushed past her without a word, stepped into the first room he came to and checked for Liz. He moved back into the hall, then into the next room. Pat, frightened, followed him. The kid went on bawling in the back room.

'Where is she?'

'I don't know.'

'She wasn't at home,' Ronnie said roughly. 'I've bin to the hospital . . . they said she was here!'

'How did you . . .'

'The police radioed the rig last night.'

'She was just depressed, Ronnie, you bein' away so much.

She's not been well. You know what she's like, you know how things get on top of her.'

'What's been going on?' Ronnie laced his powerful fingers in Pat's stringy hair.

'Nothing!' Pat cried out, terrified.

Ronnie twisted her head sideways, painfully.

'You're a worse bloody liar than she is!' he shouted.

'Ronnie, don't!' Pat screamed.

He could see he was hurting her and tried to calm himself. He let go her hair and she held her head. In the other room the kid was still howling.

'I told her the last time . . . if it happened again I'd bloody kill her.'

'Nothing's happened like that.' Pat tried to lower the tension.

'No other men?'

'There's been no one.'

'Are you sure?'

'Ronnie, I swear it.'

'Then who was the pretty boy at the hospital?' Ronnie spoke very quietly and saw the fear in Pat's face. 'The one with the chat and the flowers? A bloody social worker? They thought he was *me*!'

'I don't know.' Pat was trembling.

'Yes, you do. She tells you everything, don't she? Every dirty little detail. Turns you on, does it?' He was working himself up again.

'No . . . no!'

'What a laugh, a real giggle. Poor old Ronnie, stuck in the middle of bloody nowhere working his guts out. What a Toby, let's spend some more of his money. Yeah? Yeah? Is that the way it is, *sister-in-law*?' He was almost at breaking point.

'You're wrong, Ronnie. You've got it all wrong.'

'You dirty sluts.' He raised a massive hand to hit her. 'Who is he, Pat?'

'You're mad.'

'Who is he?' Ronnie raised his hand higher.

'You hit me, Ronnie, and I'll go to the police.'

'You bloody would an' all,' he said with disgust.

'I would – and enjoy it.'

'You phlegm.' Ronnie slowly lowered his hand and looked at Pat with utter contempt. 'I'll find out who he is. I'll find out. Then I'm goin' to spread his face on a wall!'

Ronnie moved to the front door, snatched it open and went out. He left the door wide open. Once he was gone the tension poured out of Pat. The kid was still crying in the back room. She turned and screamed at it until the veins stood out on her neck.

'Shut uuuuuuuuuuuuuuuupppppppp!'

Then she burst into tears.

Joey had been cruising the district searching for Liz. He was tired and drawn. He scanned the faces as he drove slowly past a shopping precinct, then suddenly he spotted her on the opposite side of the road. He slammed on the brakes and stopped. A van behind him blared its horn as Joey jumped out, abandoning the cab with its door open and motor running.

'Liz!' he shouted as he ran across the road. He caught up with her and spun her round to face him.

'What the hell do you think you're playing—'

The sentence foundered when Joey realised he'd made a mistake. The woman was of the same height, build and hair but it wasn't Liz.

'Sorry! Sorry, love. I thought you was . . . my mistake, sorry.'

Joey turned and ran back across the road to his cab. The van behind was having great difficulty getting round against the stream of oncoming traffic. A loaded skip lorry was stranded behind Joey's cab like a dirty orange whale. As Joey got back into his cab the skip lorry driver leaned out to give him a well-earned mouthful.

'Oi! Goofy!'

Joey slammed the door of his cab.

'Dollop 'ead!' The driver behind hadn't finished. ' 'Ad a nice 'oliday?'

Joey jammed the cab into gear and pulled away.

Ray was changing his trousers in the small but comfortable office over his club. The door opened and Detective Inspector Alex Tupper came in without knocking. This copper Ray knew only too well. About forty, slim, very fit, a dangerous face. When Tupper saw Ray with his strides in his hand he put on a mock turd burglar voice and held his bum in his hand.

'Not today, Ray.'

Ray pulled on his trousers. 'Don't you ever knock?'

Tupper obediently went back to the door and knocked. Ray zipped up the trousers, fastened the belt.

'How's yer luck?' Tupper asked.

'Fair up to now.'

Ray crossed the room to a small bar and poured out two large brandies. He held one out to Tupper, who took it.

'You little rascal,' Tupper said.

'What's up?' Ray sipped his brandy.

'I hear you've been givin' one of my team a vexing time?'

'Mr Health and Strength?' Ray was surprised. 'He's one of yours?'

'Cor . . . rect.' Tupper took a drink of his brandy.

'He never let on.'

'He's the strong silent type.'

'He's a pushy feller.'

'Very ambitious.'

'If he carries on like that he's goin' to be very unpopular.'

Tupper took another sip. 'Nice little taste.'

Ray knew the rules of the game as well as Tupper. Up to now they'd been sniffing each other out like two dogs in an alley. It was time to move forward.

'You shoppin'?' Ray asked.

'What yer got?'

'Depends.'

'Click, click, click . . .' said Tupper.

'On what *you've* got.'

'I've got Terry Connell by the plums!' Tupper said with pleasure.

'That's painful,' Ray remarked drily.

'Now you know me, Ray, I'm a very amiable man, very accommodating.'

'And very expensive.'

'That depends on how you look at it. That depends, my friend, on how far the shit's up yer neck! I mean, what premium does one place on one's liberty?' Tupper smiled.

'You do 'ave a sparkling turn of phrase, Alex.'

'Education, my son . . . a wonderful thing.'

'How much?' Ray asked.

'I've got a lot of overheads. I mean, managing this place you no doubt are quite conversant with overheads.'

'How much?' Ray ignored the bullshit.

'Two an' alf,' Tupper answered matter-of-factly.

'Do leave off. For that sort of money I know Terry'll take 'is chances.'

'He don't *have no* chances.' Tupper hardened. 'I hope you impress that upon him.'

'Someone bubbled 'im?'

'Nothing so delicate.'

'No?' Ray asked, unconvinced.

'Is that what he thinks?'

'That's what *I* think.'

'Two grand. Last offer.'

'I'll talk to 'im.'

'You do that. I'll call by tonight.' Tupper drained his glass.

'Not too early,' Ray told him.

'You know me, Mr Fox, like your good self, a creature of the night.'

Tupper took Ray's hand, deposited his empty brandy glass in it, turned and went out.

Liz sat on a bench overlooking a rundown playground, where a bunch of children were noisily enjoying the rusting equipment. Liz was deep in thought, staring blankly a few feet ahead of her at the ground. Joey appeared behind her, slipped on to the bench beside her. He made no attempt to touch her or say anything. Liz was so far away she didn't even notice him at first. He sat there patiently until she turned to him.

'You should be in bed,' he said.

Liz didn't speak. She just tried to get up and walk away but she could hardly stand.

'I've been looking for you all morning.'

'It's a bit late,' Liz muttered almost to herself.

'What?' Joey only half heard.

Liz started to walk away and Joey got up to follow.

'I never realised. I . . . I didn't think.'

'You never do, do you, Joey? I mean, think about anybody but Joey? You're like a selfish little boy who's always got to be first.'

'Come back and sit down.' Joey put an arm out to try to turn her back to the bench. She pulled away, closed her eyes to shut out the world.

'Just . . . just leave me alone, Joey!'

Liz opened her eyes and continued walking slowly. Joey

followed cautiously.

'You look done in.' Liz just walked on. 'I want to help, Liz.'

'Don't you think you've *helped* me enough?' Liz asked bitterly.

'I'm not leaving you like this. I've got the cab, let me take you home?'

'Home . . . where's that?' Liz asked scornfully.

'Your place.'

'Oh, he'd love that!'

'Who?' Joey didn't understand.

'Ronnie. The police radioed the rig last night. The company flew him by helicopter to the mainland.' Joey looked uncomfortable. 'The sister told me at five o'clock this morning. Why do you think I got out of there? That'll be the first place he'll go.'

'He don't know . . . about us?'

'He's a lot of things but he's not a bloody fool. You don't think you're the first, do you? Oh dear, poor Joey, always wants to be the first.'

'What happened last time?'

'He busted my arm and knocked three teeth out.'

'You never said nothin'?'

'There's a lot I never told you about good old Ronnie.'

'Let me take you to Pat's, then?'

'That's the second place he'll go.'

'What are you goin' to do?' Joey was getting desperate. 'Where are you goin' to go?'

'I don't know. Somewhere. What do you care anyway?'

'If I didn't care, would I be here?' Joey pleaded.

'You're just feelin' guilty.'

By now they had made their way through the park and were near where Joey's cab was parked.

'You think what you like, you've got to go somewhere. Get some rest, somethin' to eat, sort things out. Let me take you to Vinnie's, you'd be safe there.' Liz shook her head. 'Renie'll look after you, she's a darlin'. Just for tonight?'

Liz shook her head again, quickening her pace to try to get away from Joey. In the end she was almost running. Suddenly she went dizzy and had to hold on to a tree to stop herself from fainting. Joey caught up with her.

'How far d'yer think you're goin' to get? If you collapse you'll go straight back to 'ospital. The first person they'll contact will be good old Ronnie!'

George stood up. He could see that Skegg was agitated about something.

'This 'ad better be good,' George told him.

George walked Skegg away from the table into a quiet corner where they couldn't be overheard. Skegg became conspiratorial.

'There's a face lookin' for someone,' he said.

'Ain't there always?' George was impatient.

'Wants 'im bad. Bin askin' around.'

'So?'

'This someone's bin messin' around with his wife while he's bin away. I know for a fact that the someone he's lookin' for is . . .' Skegg paused for effect, '*Joey Fox*.'

The moment George Macey heard the magic name his attitude changed. 'Is it now? Fancy that!' He smiled. 'Jungle Joey?'

'I thought you'd like to know, Mr Macey,' Skegg said obsequiously.

'What's this feller like?'

'Frightening!'

'What's 'is name?'

'Ronnie Boyd.'

George knew the name and smiled.

'D'you know him, Mr Macey?'

'*Of* him. Where is he now?'

'Round the corner, in the Tons.'

Ronnie Boyd was alone at the bar drinking heavily without getting drunk. George and Frank Macey came in, spotted him easily and walked over.

'Large malt, large navy rum,' Frank said to the barmaid. 'What about you, mate?' he asked Ronnie.

'You talking to me?' Ronnie looked George and Frank over.

'Same again for 'im,' Frank ordered.

Ronnie moved away slightly to give himself room if there was going to be any trouble.

'Who are you two monkeys?' he asked belligerently.

'Easy son, we've come to do you a favour.'

George passed Ronnie his drink, a large scotch.

'There yer go,' he said. 'Hear you're lookin' for someone?'

'That any business of yours?' Ronnie was still uneasy.

'We're goin' to give 'im to yer,' George said.

Ronnie grabbed hold of the lapel of George's expensive suit.

'Listen, smiler, I ain't in the mood for a wind up!'

Ronnie looked hard but George Macey was just as hard. He looked down at Ronnie's hand on his suit.

'You're bendin' the wardrobe!' George warned coldly.

Ronnie released his grip.

'Who is he?' he asked.

'*Joey Fox.*'

Anna and Phil were sitting on the floor, watching an old film on television. The debris of a takeaway Chinese meal lay on the floor with an empty bottle of wine. Suddenly the doorbell rang.

'Damn!' Anna got up to answer it. From the hall Phil heard their voices. It was Anna's father. Phil heard him speak in a rich, urbane voice.

'We're late already, Anna.' He sounded peeved.

'I'm sorry, Daddy. I'd completely forgotten!'

'Well, hurry up.'

'You'd better go on without me,' Anna said, sounding nervous.

'But . . . you're *expected*!'

'I know, I'm sorry. I honestly did forget.'

'You only forget when it suits you . . .' His voice trailed off as Anna brought him into the room to make a cursory introduction.

'This is Philip Fox, a friend from university. This is my father, Phil.'

'Hello,' Phil said, standing up and feeling awkward. Anna's father was about sixty, dressed in immaculate black tie. He looked distinguished and very assured.

'Good evening,' he said, shaking Phil's hand very formally. 'There seems to have been a bit of a mix-up,' he said, looking Phil over.

'I've got to leave anyway,' Phil said, looking at Anna and feeling self-conscious.

'Why?' Anna asked.

'A few things to sort out before going back. Maybe I can get a lift tomorrow?'

Anna knew Phil was just trying to be tactful.

'I'm not going out, Phil. Please stay.'

Phil didn't know what to do. Anna looked at her father.

'Apologise for me,' she said.

'I will not!'

'Please, Daddy . . .'

'Your mother will be very upset.'

'*She* didn't want to go.' Anna immediately wished she hadn't said it. Her father's face clouded.

'What do you mean?'

'Nothing.'

'Then why did you say it?'

'They're *your* friends, not really *hers*,' Anna said sharply.

Her father turned and walked out of the room. Anna ran after him. 'I'm sorry . . .'

Phil could hear them arguing in the hallway, their voices getting fainter as they reached the door. Then the door slammed. After a little while Anna came back.

'It's always like that.' She was very upset. Phil crossed the room and put his arm round her to comfort her. Anna kissed him. 'I want to go to bed,' she said.

Ray Fox's white Jaguar was parked in an underground garage. Terry Connell was in the car with Ray, looking well pissed off with what Ray was telling him.

'Two grand!' Terry exclaimed.

'I knocked it down from two 'n' half.'

'Greedy bastard!'

'How much did you pull from the job?'

'Three 'n' 'alf,' Terry said, embarrassed.

'I thought you said it was a good little earner?'

'You 'ave to say that, don't yer?'

'You risk five years for three and a half grand?' Ray was amazed. 'You must want your 'ead tappin'.'

'Most of the tom was bloody Woolworths,' Terry grumbled.

'I bet that ain't what's down on the insurance claim,' Ray said sardonically.

'Probably claimin' twenty grand. Bent bastards, worse than us.'

'Well, it don't change nothin', Terry. He wants two or you're up the steps.'

'Did he say how?'

'Leave off! That slippery bastard?'

Terry was resigned. 'It'll take a couple of days to get it together.'

'Take my advice,' Ray said. 'After this leave it out for a while.'

'After this I'll be on the blackin' . . . I got to work,' Terry insisted.

'Well, use your 'ead. Stay out of his face. Work up North, anywhere but down 'ere.'

'Yeah, you're right. Thanks, Ray, anyway.'

'Don't go home until I tell yer, just in case.'

Terry opened his door and stepped out. He slammed the door and started to make his way out of the car park. There was an empty can lying around and Terry kicked his frustration out on it. Ray started the Jag and pulled away. Terry gave the can another belt as the Jag hissed past him and it went clanking away like a tin ball down the concrete.

It was dark when Vin opened the door to Pat. He recognised her from the night of the party and was surprised to see her again.

'Is Joey here?' Pat asked anxiously.

'No . . .'

'Do you know where he is?'

'No, no, I don't. What's happened?'

'I've got to find him. Warn him!'

'You'd better come in,' Vin said.

Ray Fox sat at the bar watching the club slowly filling and listening to Alan Haywood do his stuff at the piano. Haywood was doing all right. He was staying off the juice and pulling in the late night crowd.

Ray saw Alex Tupper and Hough coming towards him. Hough and Ray exchanged hard looks.

'I was expectin' you later,' Ray told Tupper. '*Alone.*'

'He has to be in bed early,' Tupper pointed to Hough. 'He's a growin' boy.'

'You're jumpin' the red a bit, aren't you, Alex?' Ray asked.

'I want you two to be pals,' Tupper said. Ray and Hough looked at each other again, a look that made the statement ludicrous. Tupper checked to be sure they couldn't be overheard, turned back to Ray.

'Well?' he asked.

'Terry ain't happy.'

'Show me a drowning man who is.' Tupper smiled.

'It'll take him a couple of days to put it together.'

'Make it Tuesday, then,' Tupper said easily.

'Where . . . here?'

'I'll let you know.'

'He can go home?'

'That's where a married man *should* be, with his family.'

Snoopy, Ray's barman, passed by and Ray caught his arm.

'Two Remies, Snoopy.'

Snoopy moved away, poured the brandies into balloon glasses.

'I told you he was a gentleman,' Tupper said to Hough.

Snoopy set the glasses down on the bar. Tupper raised his glass to Ray.

'Be lucky,' he said.

Ray held out his hand. 'That'll be fifty.'

'Fifty?' Hough couldn't believe it.

'Two large brandies . . . a pony apiece.' Ray looked at Tupper. 'Overheads,' he said.

Hough picked up his glass and put it to Ray's face. 'I ought to shove it up your nose!'

'Oh dear,' Tupper turned to Ray. 'You've got him cross again.'

He took a fistful of notes from his pocket. Hough couldn't believe his guvnor was going to pay up.

'You're givin' *him* money!'

'Shut it!' Tupper turned on Hough. Tupper peeled off five tens and slipped them to Ray. 'I like your new piano player. Nice touch, delicate hands.'

They downed their drinks and Tupper moved away from the bar with Hough at his side. 'You're pushing it, son,' he said quietly.

'What is he?' Hough sneered.

'I should hate you to find out the hard way.'

The two coppers made their way out of the club while Ray watched them from the bar. As Tupper passed Alan Haywood at the piano he stopped for a word. After a minute he walked away.

'Play "Temptation",' he said over his shoulder.

Joey got back to his flat late that night. He felt very tired as he unlocked the door, came in and switched on the light. For a few seconds he couldn't take in what he saw. The place had been wrecked, the furniture turned over and smashed. The parrot cage was mangled and the bird lay dead on the floor. Suddenly Joey was grabbed from behind and rammed against a wall so hard the breath went out of him.

'Where is she?' Ronnie Boyd spat, both hands clamped round Joey's throat so tight he was choking. 'Where's the whore?' he hissed.

Joey kicked out desperately, catching him in the balls.

Ronnie gasped, the hands dropped away. Joey moved across the room, putting some of the smashed furniture between them. Joey held his throat and tried to breathe, looking at him.

'I'm goin' to bruise you, pretty boy!' Ronnie said.

Joey tried to get to the door but Ronnie cut him off and grabbed him with one hand. Joey nutted him on the bridge of the nose and got away again.

'She's gone,' Joey said.

'I'll find her – I found you!' Ronnie picked up a chair and hurled it. He made a sudden dive at Joey, who just managed to get out of the way. He moved quickly to the door to snatch it open but Ronnie was up and on him. As he grabbed Joey by the hair and dragged him back into the wrecked room there was the noise of someone kicking in the front door of the flat. Joey wrenched away in a desperate attempt to get free, leaving a clutch of his hair in Ronnie's hand.

Ronnie looked up as the door to the room swung open. In filed Billy, Vin and Kenny. He backed off to give himself space to fight, picked up a chair and tore off a leg. Billy took control.

'Put it down, Ronnie,' Billy said calmly.

'Who are you?'

'Family.'

'Come on, then, come on.' Ronnie waved the chair leg club at them. None of the Fox family moved.

'Come on, I'll have the lot of you!'

'No you won't,' Billy said quietly.

'Try me, old man!' he threatened.

Billy let two feet of lead pipe slide down his jacket sleeve, where it had been hidden.

'I'll bust yer 'ead open!' Billy nodded towards Vin who was tooled up with a length of pipe too. 'If I don't get yer, he will.'

Billy nodded at Joey. 'I ain't makin' excuses for 'im, son. He's a dirty little slag. He done wrong and he knows it. But it takes two. Your missus, it ain't the first time, is it?' Billy looked at Ronnie for a reaction. 'Is it?' he insisted.

'I warned her,' Ronnie said.

'I know. Her sister told me.'

'That slut!'

Billy gestured round the wrecked room, almost approvingly. 'Joey asked for this. I know how you feel. I'd feel the same, but there's an end to it.'

Ronnie pointed with the chair leg at Joey who was as white as a sheet. 'I want *him*!'

'You take *one* Fox, you take us all! I told you, we're *family*!' Billy had stopped persuading now. He was ready to fight.

Ronnie gripped his chair leg and sized up his chances.

Billy, Vin, and Kenny looked back at him, rock hard faces.

Ronnie dropped his club, turned to Joey. 'I'll find her,' he said.

'It weren't her fault,' Joey croaked.

'I'll find her,' Ronnie repeated firmly. He pushed past Billy, then past Vin. Kenny was by the door. Ronnie glared at him as if trying to photograph the face. Kenny, half his size, glared back without a glimmer of fear, as he left.

Ray Fox sat at his desk with the lights out, his tie undone and feet up on the desk. Street light splashed through the window. Down in the club Alan Haywood was playing 'Misty'. Ray pulled the five tens Tupper gave him from his pocket. He looked at the notes, screwed them into a ball and dropped them into the ashtray on his desk. Then he set fire to them with his lighter and watched them burn.

SEVEN

RENIE was seeing her two girls, Sammy and Karen, off to school when the totter's cart passed her house in Battersea. The totter was a strange-looking old boy with long grey hair, dressed in an ankle-length black coat. The cart was a wreck, with a long wooden box loaded on it. It was drawn by a bony, half-starved, ancient horse. As he drove by the totter tilted his head back like a strange bird of prey and let go a strangled croak of a street cry. The girls, frightened of him, ran up the road. Renie watched him, suspicion written over her face. He stood up in the cart and bowed to her very formally.

Renie went back into the house, walked through to the back and looked in the garden to check that Andy was all right. He'd been playing with a puppy Vin had just bought for the kids but now Renie couldn't see him anywhere. She looked round the garden again; he had to be there *somewhere*. At the bottom of the garden she noticed an old pram, discarded years ago, propped against the fence. Renie ran back to the house.

Andy knew he wasn't allowed in the street on his own, but when the puppy squeezed through a small hole in the fence he'd used the pram to go over the top. The puppy led Andy quite a dance, past the totter's cart at the end of the road and through some backstreets. On the junction with a main road the puppy darted across and Andy watched as a car narrowly missed it. Andy checked the traffic and crossed cautiously. Without his hearing aid the traffic was silent and extra dangerous.

Renie ran frantically up the street outside her house, asking any passers-by if they'd seen Andy, but no luck. In the next street she saw the totter and ran up to his cart.

'Have you seen a kid, with a puppy?' she panted. The totter smiled his mad, toothless smile but said nothing. 'A boy . . . 'bout nine, with a dog?' Renie asked again.

The totter barked like a dog, then smiled again.

'Just now?' Renie didn't give up.

'Right missus.' The totter finally spoke.

'You have?'

'Certainly.'

'Which way did he go?'

'Past . . . towards . . . down.' The totter pointed and Renie ran off in that direction.

The puppy ran into the grounds of a small factory with Andy on its heels, almost catching up. He cornered it in the vehicle yard, picking it up to cuddle it while the puppy licked his face. A heavy lorry was reversing hard. Andy's back was turned, the puppy cradled in his arms. Just in time a young secretary coming out of the office block saw the lorry bearing down on the child and screamed at the top of her lungs. The driver, a big man in his forties, heard the scream and smashed on the brakes. The lorry ground to a stop only a few feet from Andy. The secretary ran over to him. The driver got down, grabbed him and started to shake him angrily.

'You stupid little – I could've killed you!' he shouted. 'What you doin' muckin' around in here anyway?' The driver shook him again when Andy didn't seem to respond. 'I'm talkin' to you!'

Andy tried to speak, his mouth moving to fit itself round unknown words, but all he could do was grunt.

'What's the matter with you? You a bloody moron?'

'Stop it, Reg,' the secretary shouted. 'Can't you see, he must be deaf?'

Renie appeared in the distance at the factory gate. When she saw Andy her face flooded with relief and she ran over. She bent down to the boy, who was sobbing but still holding the puppy tightly in his arms.

'What happened?'

'I bloody near killed him, that's what happened!'

'It wasn't Reg's fault,' the young secretary intervened.

'No . . . no, of course not.'

'It would 'ave bin your fault, lady,' Reg said aggressively.

The secretary tried to calm him down.

'What's he doin' out on the street with a bloody dog, no collar or lead? Bloody deaf, dumb and simple?'

'He's not simple,' Renie said defensively.

'He ain't too bloody bright, is he?' Reg turned abruptly back to his lorry and got into the cab.

'Shook him up a bit,' the secretary explained. 'He's a decent bloke.'

Renie put her arm round Andy's shoulder and started to walk him back to the gate. Behind them Reg was turning the lorry round. He started to drive towards them. By now he'd calmed down enough to be ashamed of what he'd said.

'Where d'you live?' he called from his cab.

'Not far.'

'Want a lift?'

Renie could see he was trying to apologise. 'It's all right, thanks.'

'I've got a boy that age,' Reg said. He drove the lorry on out through the gates. Renie bent down so that her face was on a level with Andy's.

'All right?' She pointed to the ear where his hearing aid should be. 'You must wear it.'

Andy dropped his head but Renie raised it so that he could read her lips.

'Then people can *see* you're deaf. All right?'

Andy nodded his head. Renie gave him a little comforting hug and walked him and the puppy out of the gate.

At the gym in the Thomas A'Beckett, Kenny was in the last stages of preparation for his fight with Charlie Locke. Eddie and Maxi were working him through a series of exercises while Billy looked on. Maxi held his feet down while Kenny did reverse sit-ups. Eddie went through their routine for the morning.

'Warm up . . . do three shadow, one speed ball, three skip.'

Kenny grunted with exertion.

'No more sparrin', Kenny,' Maxi said.

Kenny nodded. 'Rest day tomorrow.'

'Don't you forget,' Maxi joked. 'No nookie tonight, not tomorrow night neither.'

'What makes you think we do it at night, Maxi?' Kenny asked, breathing heavily.

'You'll end up in the Screws of the World!'

Billy slipped out of the room and walked downstairs, passing a notice on the wall that read 'Pugilism not Vandalism'. The bar of the Beckett had a magic atmosphere in spite of the cracked plastic seats and worn carpets. Framed photographs of fighters covered the walls, there was a stage in the corner and the bar curled round, two hundred and forty degrees. Billy crossed to the bar.

'Gettin' hot up there, Billy?' asked the barmaid.

'Fancied a swift 'alf, duck,' Billy said with a smile.

Bette was waiting for a taxi, carrying several heavy packages. On the pavement beside her was a covered parrot cage. She was beautiful in a kooky way, with ultra fashionable clothes in the Zandra Rhodes style and an individual way of wearing them that went with her hair and make-up. She hailed a cab on the opposite side of the road and it did a swift U-turn to pull up alongside her. Joey was at the wheel.

'Want a hand?' he asked. Bette started to gather up all her bits and pieces. She dropped a package and bent down to retrieve it. Joey got out and helped load the things into the cab. The parrot grumbled and swore in its cage as Joey handed it in.

'Thanks,' Bette said. Joey closed the passenger door, got in the cab and started up.

Joey watched in his mirror as Bette fitted a cigarette into an ivory holder.

'African Grey?' he asked over his shoulder.

'Sorry, what?'

'The bird . . . the parrot . . . is it an African Grey?'

'No. Green Amazon. Krapp.'

'I beg your pardon?'

'His name. Krapp.'

'They do, don't they?'

'K . . . R . . . A . . . double P. You know, the Beckett character.'

'Oh yeah. Yeah, of course, the Beckett character,' Joey bluffed. 'I had an African Grey, Popeye. P . . . O . . . P . . . E . . . Y . . . E. You know, the cartoon character?'

'I've got three,' said Bette. 'Krapp, a Scarlet Macaw called Asthma Joe and a Sulphur-Crested Cockatoo called Albina Terrasina Beak.'

'You're a girl for names, aren't you?'

'They're important,' Bette said. 'A name is a kind of face.'

'Never thought of it that way,' Joey said. He'd never met anyone quite like Bette before . . .

Twenty minutes later the cab pulled up outside a big Edwardian house in Notting Hill.

'Would you give me a hand in?' Bette asked.

'I'll take the cage.' Joey switched off the ignition. He followed Bette into the house. He wasn't quite expecting what he saw. The hallway was filled with stuffed animals.

'Jesus!' Joey said, looking round.

Bette slammed the front door, pointed to a side room.

'Through there.' She laughed. 'Not Jesus – the parrot.'

Joey carried the cage into a big room. It was weird, with black painted walls, floor and ceiling. There was very little furniture, brightly coloured cushions everywhere and erotic paintings. The other two parrots were in this room, the Scarlet Macaw on an open perch and the cockatoo in a large cage.

'Put him over there.' Bette pointed.

Joey put the cage down while she dumped her packages, then she came over to the cage and uncovered it. Krapp gave out a long wolf whistle.

'There you go, Krappy. Home.'

Joey looked around the room in amazement. His eyes settled on a naughty painting.

'Blimey!'

'Do you like it?'

'I could get nicked for just thinking about that. What d'yer do? I mean, what are you?'

'I design clothes.'

An enormous Irish wolfhound clacked across the wooden floor.

'That a dog or a donkey?'

'This is Lop Lop.' Bette put her arms round the dog's neck and kissed it.

'Again?'

'The dog superior, Lop Lop. She gave it another kiss as it stood docilely.

'Isn't he just too much?' she asked admiringly.

'He's certainly enough!' Joey said.

At the Beckett, Kenny finished training and took a shower with Maxi. While Kenny shampooed his hair Maxi sang, very badly. Eddie poked his head round the dilapidated stone shower.

'Watch him, Kenny, he pisses in the shower!'

'I close me eyes!' Maxi tried to sound offended.

Eddie moved out of the shower room, through a small anteroom used for massage and into the gym. Billy was standing alone by the big window, staring at the traffic below in the Old Kent Road, lost in thought.

'Penny for 'em,' said Eddie.'

'Ain't sure they're worth it.'

'Somethin' on your mind, Billy?'

'Just somethin' someone said.' He shrugged. 'About maybe bringin' Kenny on too soon?'

'What do you think?'

'To be honest, I'm not sure.'

'Kenny's sure. He knows. You see, Billy, it doesn't matter what we think. It's what's in Kenny's mind that matters. Kenny's wanted Charlie Locke for a long time. I could have talked him out of it, put it off for a twelvemonth, matched him with a couple of useful Yanks. But Kenny would know, he'd know I was bottling. And what would that do for him, for his confidence in himself . . . in me?' Eddie paused. 'Kenny's the best prospect I've ever had. God willing he could be a world champion one day and I don't make that sort of claim lightly. But the day you start dodging fighters like Charlie Locke is the day you start looking backwards.'

Billy put an arm round Eddie's shoulder and gave him a squeeze.

Joey nosed around Bette's house. He found himself in a room with a shower and sauna bath. He opened the door to the sauna and hot air blasted out. He closed the door as Bette's voice came from behind him.

'I wondered where you'd got to.'

'I was having a nose.' Joey was embarrassed.

'You've seen a sauna before.'

'No, I haven't. I'm a workin' class hero. It's a tin bath in front of the fire on Fridays.'

Bette laughed. 'You've never had a sauna?'

'Scout's honour.'

Bette opened the door to check the temperature. 'Well, now's your chance.'

'Really?' Joey was like a school boy with a treat.

'Be my guest.'

Joey took a quick look inside the sauna. 'It's out of order, isn't it?'

'Out of order?'

'Somethin' missin'.'

'What do you mean?'

'Where's the big butch blonde who gives yer snake bites to the waist an' beats yer 'alf to death with a hedge?'

Bette laughed. 'There's towels in that drawer.' She went out. Joey stripped and took a place inside the sauna. Five minutes later he was lying on a towel, sweat pouring out of him. The door of the sauna opened. Joey looked up and nearly fell off the slatted wooden bench. Bette was standing in the doorway, carrying a tray with a Chinese tea set on it. She was stark naked.

'I hope you like jasmine tea.'

EIGHT

IT was a perfect day for a trip on the river, warm and sunny. The boat was only half full and Andy was in his element. He sat on a seat by himself, loving every minute, waving to people on the bank as the boat moved upriver towards Teddington. Vin and Renie were at the back of the boat, keeping an eye on him.

'I reckon he'll eat his tea,' Vin said. He'd come back from the office to get some papers and Renie told him about the incident with the puppy. On impulse Vin decided to take the afternoon off and give the boy a treat.

'If you could've seen his little face this morning,' Renie said.

'Forget it, love. He has.'

Andy moved up the boat and watched the coxswain carefully steering the pleasure launch through the river traffic. Vin settled back in his seat to enjoy the warm sun.

'This is the ticket: no telephones, no clients wantin' everythin' yesterday. I could sling it all in tomorrow.'

'Do you mean that, Vin?'

'Too right I do.'

'I'm being serious.'

'You are, aren't you?' Vin sensed something in her voice. 'Got somethin' on yer mind?'

'No, no it's nothing.' Renie was dismissive.

'Come on, love.'

'You might not like it.'

'I'll soon let you know if I don't.'

'I'm beginning to hate London,' Renie said after a long pause. 'It's changed,' she went on. 'It isn't like it was when we were kids. It's dying slowly, bit by bit.'

Vin took off his sunglasses and listened carefully.

'No one laughs out loud any more,' Renie said. 'No one whistles. It's all grab, grab, grab, money, money, money. Too many cars, too many drunks, too many foreigners, filth everywhere. It isn't a place to raise kids any more, they never get the chance to *be* kids, not like we were, anyway.'

Vin just looked at her. He said nothing.

'I've got this . . . this dream, I suppose you'd call it. I've had it a long while now. You an' me an' the kids, house by the sea, little business. Just think . . . think about it, Vin. It could be like this every day. Our friends could visit. You wouldn't have to work all the hours God sends.' Renie laughed at herself. 'It's *just* a dream. There's the firm, the family, the house. We're tied to London. Maybe one day—'

Vin put his hand on hers. 'All the times we've talked,' he said. 'You've never said, never mentioned . . .'

'I didn't want you to think I was unhappy. I wasn't, Vin, I'm not now. It's just, we all have our private thoughts, don't we? I mean that's part of living, part of coping. I didn't want you to worry.' Renie tried to laugh it all off. 'It's the water. Does things to me.'

Phil Fox stood at the pay telephone in the university corridor. Students moved up and down behind him. He had a pile of two pence pieces in front of him and waited while Vin's number rang. He pushed the first coin in the slot.

'Vin . . . Vin, it's Phil.'

'When you comin' down, Phil?'

'I'm not.'

'What d'you mean?'

'I can't make the fight,' Phil said simply.

'Don't be bloody daft! Of course you're comin'.'

'No, Vin, no I'm not.'

'But I've got your ticket. You've never missed, none of us have.'

'I know. I'm sorry.'

'Sorry's no good, Phil!'

'I can't make it.'

'Why not?'

'I've got too much work.'

'Don't give me that old fanny.' Vin was getting worked up. 'I'll come up and fetch you Tuesday afternoon, run you back Tuesday night. What is it, a few hours at most?'

'It's no good, Vin. I'm not coming.'

'What about Kenny? It's the hardest fight he's ever had. He needs us all.'

'The rest of you will be there.'

'You're Kenny's *brother*!'

'All right, I'll ring Kenny.'

'No! Don't do that.'

'Why not?'

'Use yer bloody 'ead. I thought you was supposed to be the bright boy, the intellectual. He really don't need this sort of number on his rest day. Look, think it over. Ring me back, reverse the charges.'

'There's nothing to think over, Vin.'

'You selfish little bastard!' Vin said, but Phil slammed down the receiver.

'Phil?'

Vin realised that Phil had rung off. He waited by the phone, expecting him to call back. When nothing happened, Vin slammed his fist angrily down on top of the telephone.

Billy's car zoomed up the motorway, eating up the miles. He was alone at the wheel and kept his foot well down on the pedal. He was fond of all his boys, they each had a special place in his heart. But Phil had always been something a bit different. There was an extra dimension to the boy, a quality Billy admired and was proud of but it made Phil difficult to get close to. Sometimes, Billy thought as he belted the car along the road, Phil just bloody irritated the hell out of him. It was as if the extra gifts God had given him made him more unpredictable, even downright awkward, at times. Anyway, Billy thought, he'd have him sorted pretty soon about Kenny's fight.

The car arrived at the grounds of the university and Billy drove through the maze of internal roads, looking for a place to park. It was all unfamiliar to him, he'd never visited Phil before. Now he came to think of it, he wasn't sure why not.

Eventually he found somewhere to park and walked around asking for directions. He ended up walking to the library, then he had a bit of luck. Anna was just passing in the opposite direction. She recognised him at once although they'd never met. She went up to him as he reached the door of the building.

'Excuse me,' Anna said, putting a hand on his shoulder. 'Are you Mr Fox?'

'That's right, duck.' Billy was surprised.

'Phil's father? I've seen your photograph in Phil's room.' She smiled.

*

Vin, Ray and Joey were having a drink in Albert's pub. Vin was telling them what had happened.

'When I told Billy, he went barmy,' said Vin. 'Got in his motor and shot up there. Connie tried to stop him goin', you know how she is about Phil, but Billy give her a right tellin' off.'

Joey looked thoughtful. 'There's somethin' up with Phil,' he said. 'I don't know what it is.'

'All them soapy sods he's stuck with,' Vin suggested. 'Hair down to their arses, dirty feet, communists – bleedin' parasites, ain't done a decent day's graft between 'em!'

'I reckon it's that bird of 'is,' Ray said.

'What bird?'

'He's got this little sort tucked away off Sloane Square.'

Vin looked at Joey, who shrugged, then turned back to Ray.

'How long have you known this?'

'He asked me not to say nothin'.' Ray realised he should have kept his mouth shut.

'The randy little—' Joey started.

'What's she like?' Vin wanted to know.

'Never met her.' Ray leaned forward on the bar. 'From what Phil says, she sounds a madam. Loaded. Her old boy's a stockbroker.'

'Bit out of his class, ain't she?' Joey asked.

'You can talk!' Vin said. 'Saunas, china tea, bleedin' great 'ouse!'

Joey was offended. 'Bette's different, at least she *earned* what she's got.'

The door to the bar opened and Dave Dury came in. He stood just inside the door, checking faces and tugging at the cuffs of his shirt which were held together by half sovereign cufflinks. Everything about Dury, from his expensive haircut and manicure to his highly polished Italian shoes and heavy gold jewellery, screamed money but no taste. He was about thirty, wearing thick-framed glasses and an expensive suit. There was something vicious, almost feminine about him that made him look very dangerous. Dury came over to the bar.

' 'Ello, Ray.'

'Dave. What you doin' this way?'

'Slummin'.'

Ray introduced his brothers. They nodded to each other, but Vin in particular didn't take to Dury.

'Ready for another little slurp?' Dury asked. Before they

could answer he called down the bar to Albert. 'Nurse!' he shouted.

Albert turned, gave Dury a hard look and came along the bar. Dury pointed to the glasses. 'Large ones,' he ordered. 'An' I'll have a gin and Angostura.'

He took out a leather cigar case from his inside pocket and a gold Dunhill. Ray was still wondering what brought him here.

'You're lookin' on top, Dave?'

'If you've got it, flaunt it,' Dury replied. 'You should see the new wheels. Maroon Corniche convertible.'

'I'm glad you're buying British,' Ray remarked lightly.

'Nothin' quite like a Rolls-Royce. It's class, innit?' He paused, then spoke quietly. 'I hear young Terry Connell 'ad a bit of argy bargy?'

'That's all tucked away.'

'I heard. Nicely, nicely.' He patted Ray's back, gestured towards Vin and Joey. 'Don't say much, do they?'

Albert arrived with the drinks. Dury took out a thick wad of notes held with a gold clip, peeled off a twenty and tossed it on the counter. Albert took it and turned away to the till. Joey raised his glass. 'Cheers,' he said to Dury.

'Good 'ealth.' Dury put his money away and picked up his drink. 'We've met before?' he asked Joey.

'Don't think so. Might have picked you up in my cab.'

'How's your Kenny?' Dury turned to Ray.

'Very fit.' Joey answered the question.

'Dave's a big fan of Charlie Locke,' Ray said quickly.

'Oh really. He's goin' to need a big fan,' Joey said.

'I'm sorry to say, gentlemen, but Charlie is a touch too tasty for your kid. A different class.'

'Class?' Joey was quick to rise. 'Charlie Locke? 'E couldn't even spell it.'

'We won't have to wait long to find out,' Ray said, trying to edge Joey away from a confrontation, but Dury began to recite Locke's impressive record. 'Twenty-three fights, twenty-two wins, fourteen of 'em on tens.'

'Most of them were cripples,' Joey retorted.

'They was after Charlie 'ad finished with them.'

'Tell you what's goin' to happen,' Joey said with relish. 'Kenny's goin' to whack Lockie, then early next year he's goin' to take the British title. Then he's goin' to spank that greasy Spaniard for the European. Then . . . then he's goin' to get a crack at the world title, an' we're all goin' to buzz across to Rio and watch 'im give it to Carillo. Bosh!'

Dury looked at Ray. 'He's got a very vivid imagination.'

'Classy Charlie's got two chances tomorrow.' Joey was obsessive on the subject of Kenny's career. ' 'Alf a chance and *no* chance.'

'You want to put yer money where yer mouth is, cocker?' Joey was coming on too strong, Dury was getting cross.

'It'll be like robbin' a man blind.'

'How much?'

'How much?' Joey asked back.

'Name it.'

'A hundred.'

Dury laughed and blew cigar smoke at Joey. 'The last of the big spenders.'

'Two.'

'Ease off, Joey,' warned Ray.

'The man wants to give his money away. How can I lose?'

'You can *always* lose, Joey,' Vin said quietly.

'That's nice. That's very nice,' Joey said. 'I'm glad Kenny isn't here to listen to you two undertakers!' He turned defiantly to Dury. 'A *grand*!'

'Joey!' Vin exclaimed.

'That's a lot of tips, taxi driver,' Dury smiled.

'Leave it, Joey,' advised Ray.

'Two ter one?' Dury offered.

'Even money,' Joey said grimly.

'I'm offerin' twos and you want even money?'

'I'm a gentleman.'

'You're a berk!'

Ray glanced at Vin, but they knew it had gone too far to stop.

'Poop or get off the pot,' Joey told Dury.

'You're on, taxi driver. A grand, even money.' Dury finished his drink. He looked at Vin's, still untouched on the bar.

'You ain't thirsty?'

'I'm savin' it to celebrate tomorrow night.'

Dury turned to Ray. 'A pair of wags, your brothers, Raymond.'

'Fancy you just droppin' in, the night before the fight,' observed Vin.

'I like to put myself about a bit.'

'So I've 'eard,' Vin said drily.

'Is that supposed to mean somethin'?'

'Everythin' means somethin'.'

Ray reached out for Dury's empty glass to buy him a drink but Dury put his hand over Ray's.

'I'll have it at the club, later. I've got a bit of pressing business.' He looked at Joey. 'You have that dough waitin' for me Wednesday morning. I get up early.'

Dury, cigar stuck between his teeth, walked out. Vin picked up the drink Dury had bought him, leaned over the bar and poured it down the sink. Albert came over to the Foxes.

'Gin and Angostura . . . that's a tart's drink innit, Albert?'

'Don't let the bins and the manicure fool you,' said Ray. 'He'd cut your heart out and make you eat it for a joke. You've got a big mouth, Joey.'

'And he's a flash git!'

'If Kenny loses—'

'Kenny's goin' to win!'

'If he don't, you'd better have that dough under your pillow!'

Billy and Anna had been waiting over an hour in Phil's bed-sitter. The room was filled with books. They overflowed from shelves, chairs, the bed itself, into piles on the floor. Sellotaped on the walls were posters of Samuel Beckett, Max Ernst and Laurel and Hardy.

This was the first time Billy had been in Phil's other world. He browsed through the titles of the books, mostly philosophy, economics and politics. He realised for the first time that Phil had been leading two lives, this one and the one he shared with the family when he came home. Phil had been careful not to let this one intrude into his family relations.

Anna was sitting in a big old armchair with the stuffing spewing out of it, smoking and checking her watch. She knew Billy's visit meant something important.

At last they heard footsteps and stood up to face the door. Phil came in, looking at them in surprise. He closed the door and faced Billy. 'You shouldn't have come, Pop. It isn't going to change anything.'

'We're going back together, tonight,' Billy said firmly.

'I told Vin.'

'I know what you told Vinnie.'

'I'm not coming.'

Billy tried to persuade him. 'No one's said nothin' to Kenny.

Not yet, he need never know.'

'Stop it, Pop, stop it. You're blackmailing me.'

'Blackmailing my own son!'

'I'm twenty-six years old, Pop. I'm not a little kid any more.' 'Well, you're acting like one.'

'Just because I don't want to do something you and the rest of the family want?'

'Why don't you want to see Kenny fight? You've never missed a fight. Why?'

'It's not a matter of not wanting to. You don't understand.'

'Make me understand. I've driven a hundred and twenty miles, spent hours looking for you. I think you owe me some sort of explanation.'

'It's very simple . . .' Phil started. He sounded patronising.

'Oh good, that's good, 'cos I'm a very *simple* person.'

'I didn't mean it to sound like that,' Phil protested too late.

'Look, son, just forget you're a very clever feller. You're talkin' to me now, to Billy, Pop, just tell me the truth.'

Phil spoke quickly. 'There's a lecture tomorrow night . . . the same time as Kenny's fight. A professor from Moscow University. Eighty-one, the most brilliant in his field. He's giving one lecture here, one in Dublin. It's probably the only time I'll get the chance to hear him, maybe meet him. Two days ago I got an invitation from a professor here who couldn't go himself.'

'You never said anything,' Anna said.

'I wasn't sure what I wanted to do.' Phil stared at her, then turned back to Billy.

'Like you said, son, it's very simple. You had to make a decision between this,' Billy gestured at all the books, 'and your family.'

'No! That's not it, that's not it at all!' Phil said angrily.

'Well what then?'

'I had to make a choice, *yes*. But not between *this*, as you call it, and my *family*. It was simply between one of Kenny's fights and the only chance I'll ever get to see this man!'

'I'll try to explain that to Kenny,' Billy said as he prepared to leave.

'You're not even trying to understand.'

Billy didn't even look at Phil. He turned to Anna.

'Nice to meet you, Anna.'

'I'm sorry,' she said.

'What are *you* sorry about?' Phil asked her.

Billy started to leave.

'You can't just leave like this,' said Phil.

'I've got a long drive. It's late and I'm tired.'

Phil put himself between Billy and the door. 'I've spent all day convincing myself I'm right. All day wandering around and thinking about it.'

'You're not expectin' sympathy, are you?'

'You know how much I love Kenny.'

'Yeah,' Billy said flatly.

'All of you. I'm sorry. Tell Kenny, I'm sorry,' Phil pleaded.

'Sorry?' Billy said. 'Tits on a bull, son. Useless. You're saying sorry before anyone's got hurt. That ain't lovin' someone, that ain't carin' about them. That's just selfish, that's not family, that's not *our* way. You know that, you know better. You're sayin' sorry when you know it's down to you, it doesn't have to happen. But you go to your Russian's lecture. And when I have to tell Kenny you're not comin' I'll say . . . he was very sorry, Kenny. Tell Kenny I'm sorry, he said. Tits on a bull!' Billy was really upset. His face was drawn and for once he looked his full age.

Fifteen minutes later Billy was driving back to London. Phil sat beside him, deep in thought. He'd given way and he hated himself for it. More, he hated Billy just at that moment for knowing all the time that he could impose his will, in the sacred cause of the family. Not just on Phil, on any of them. Phil suddenly sat bolt upright.

'Pull over,' he said. 'Stop the car.' Phil grabbed the steering wheel and yanked it over.

Billy knocked his hand off and pulled the car into the side of the road. 'What's the matter with you?'

'You tell Kenny I'm sorry. I don't care who it's down to or how it sounds!'

Phil snatched open the door and got out of the car, his holdall in his hand. He started running back towards the university and disappeared into the blackness. Billy got out, stared up the road and called just once.

'Phil!' Billy's voice drifted out into the darkness, very faint.

Billy got back in the car and drove away towards London, the tail lights slowly melting into the night.

NINE

The weigh-in was held in the crowded gym at the Thomas A'Beckett. There were the boxers' retinues, families and friends, as well as sports journalists, boxing business people, the undercard fighters and all the hangers-on of the boxing world.

Some people had brought drinks up from the bar below. There was a lot of noise, laughter and cigar smoke.

A beautiful pair of old weighing scales with polished brass weights had been set up close to the open side of the sparring ring. Kenny, stripped to his underpants, climbed on.

'Fox: ten stones six and one quarter pounds,' an official called out.

Maxi was waiting with Kenny's clothes as Charlie Locke climbed on the scales. The official adjusted the weights and checked.

'Locke: ten stones seven pounds.'

There was a rueful cheer. Locke was bang on the maximum limit. A small feller with a dodgy beezer called Conk sidled up to Eddie.

'They've 'ad 'im in the sauna for the last 'alf hour,' Conk said.

'Thought he looked a bit pink.'

Maxi came up to Eddie looking pleased. 'He's had trouble makin' it,' he said in a low voice.

There was a bit of gamesmanship between Kenny and Charlie as they got dressed side by side.

'I've already beat you twice,' Charlie said.

'Long time ago, Charlie. We was amateurs. You're an old man now.'

'I beat you three times, you're mine. For keeps, put you on my shelf.'

Charlie's manager, Arthur Graham, approached Eddie.

'He's looking sweet, Eddie.'

'They both are.'

'Pity they ain't matched for the title.'

Billy and Ray Fox had been watching the proceedings from a distance. Dave Dury came up to Ray with Mel, his minder.

'Where's the taxi driver?'

'He was comin',' Ray said.

'He's out earnin' some wages,' Mel said snidely.

'He's goin' to need some,' Dury sneered. 'He pushes easy?' he asked Ray.

'Joey? Yeah, he do.' Ray took the drink from Mel's hand and downed it. 'But I don't!' He tossed the empty glass back to Mel, who fumbled to catch it.

Joey and Bette were in bed. Her bedroom was as bizarre as the rest of the house.

'What's the time?'

'Who cares?' Bette asked lazily.

Joey reached out for his clothes on the floor and Bette bit his back. He grabbed his trousers, searched his pockets for his watch, found it.

'I've missed the bloody weigh-in!'

He jumped out of bed and started to get dressed.

'Oh my! I *am* sorry,' Bette said sarcastically.

'I didn't mean—'

'Just drop in any time you're passing.'

'Don't go moody on me,' Joey said sharply.

'I'm not one of your little South London scrubbers, Joey!'

'I *always* go to the weigh-in.'

Bette started to pull his shirt out of his trousers. 'If you've missed it, you've missed it,' she insinuated.

'You are a very rude lady.'

'I want another bite.'

Joey pulled away, got up from the bed and started to put on his socks and shoes. 'I'll see you tonight.'

'Maybe.'

'But you said—'

'I said *maybe*!'

'Suit yerself.' Joey shrugged. 'I ain't goin' to beg you.' As he walked to the door Bette threw a pillow at him. He turned round.

Bette smiled. 'I hate you.'

Joey grinned, threw the pillow back and went out.

Kenny had an afternoon sleep before getting his stuff together for the fight. He got up for a cup of tea with Connie and Billy, then Nan arrived and they all sat together in the living room.

Nan was as anxious as the rest of them. 'How are you feeling?' she asked.

'Really good.' Kenny winked at her.

'Bit of bad news, Kenny,' Billy said casually.

'Oh?'

'Phil phoned while you was napping. He's gone down with that bloody bug goin' round. He waited till the last minute to see if it cleared up.'

'He's not comin'?' Kenny was disappointed.

Connie joined in the story. 'He was ever so upset.'

Kenny was concerned for his brother. 'Poor old Phil. He's never missed a fight.'

'He's pig sick about it,' Billy said. 'Sends you his best. He wants us to phone . . . after the fight.'

'I'll have a quick word with him.'

'No!' Billy said quickly.

'He must be feelin' lousy not to make it.'

Connie spoke quickly. 'He was tryin' to get some sleep, the doctor give him something.'

'Doctor? He's all right? I mean, it's just a virus?'

'The old green apple quickstep,' Billy said reassuringly.

There was a ring on the doorbell, announcing Eddie's arrival. While Kenny packed his gear, Nan came up to the bedroom for a last word. She put her arms round him.

'Sorry about Phil,' she said.

'Yeah. Well, that's the way things go sometimes.'

'Are you very disappointed?'

'More for Phil than for me. He's never missed a fight, not even when I was an amateur. He was lookin' forward to this one special.'

'I know, still, we'll all be there.' She gave him a kiss. 'Good luck, love.'

That night Albert's boozer was packed. A lot of the regulars were going to be at Kenny's fight. The Fox family, dressed up, were having a drink before setting off. They were laughing together at some crack of Billy's when the door of the bar opened and Bette came in, looking quite simply amazing. She was dressed from head to toe in black leather and heavily made up. All eyes in the pub swivelled towards her. There was a moment of astonished silence.

'Oh no!' Joey moaned to himself.

As she spotted him and made her way through the crowded pub, Ray whispered to Joey. 'Is this it?'

'Where's 'er horse?' Vin asked.

'Sorry I'm a bit late, Joey.' Bette seemed unconcerned by the impression she'd made. Joey awkwardly made introductions to the family. Bette shook hands all round, while the punters in the pub still couldn't take their eyes off her. Nan suddenly realised who she was. 'You're Bette Green?'

'That's right.'

'The dress designer.' Nan was very excited and turned to Renie.

'I saw you on television,' said Renie.

'Why didn't you tell us, Joey?' Nan asked.

' 'Cos she never told me.' Joey was still puzzled by the adulation.

'What?'

'You was famous,' Joey said grudgingly.

'I'm not,' Bette laughed, self-mocking. 'I just make ridiculous gear for ridiculous birds whose fellers pay ridiculous prices for it. It's all a great big joke!' She did a twirl to let the punters get an eyeful. 'I mean, you have to be ridiculous to want to wear something like this.'

'Good for you, gel,' Billy roared with laughter. 'What d'you want to drink?'

'A pint of bitter.'

Vin didn't think she was serious.

'In a thin glass?' he asked with a touch of sarcasm.

She pointed to the pint Vin held in his hand. 'I bet you a fiver I can drink a pint faster than you can.'

Vin still wasn't sure she was serious. None of them had met anyone quite like her.

'He thinks I'm joking,' she said after a moment.

'You're on,' Vin decided quickly, then turned to the bar. 'Two pints of Pig's, Albert.'

The Fox clan had taken to Bette. They gathered round to watch as Albert set up the two pints.

'I'll take a quid on the filly,' Billy offered.

Bette approved. 'Now there's a sportsman.'

'I'll have some of that, Pop.' Ray took him up.

Bette and Vin picked up their glasses and stood poised.

'You start us, Billy,' said Bette.

'On the count of three, okay? One . . . two . . . two and a half . . .' There was laughter, the whole pub was watching. 'Three!'

Bette downed her pint like a twenty-stone prop forward just out of a hot bath. Vin was no slouch but Bette beat him, slamming her empty glass down on the bar. The whole pub cheered.

At the venue the ring was ready. The hall was deserted and only a white cat threaded its way delicately between the rows of empty seats.

In the changing room, Maxi was taping Kenny's hands and telling him a story to keep his mind relaxed.

'What 'e don't know is that I'm up there before 'em, hiding under the bed. Anyway, up they come . . . and off come the bleedin' lot, an' they're at it!'

Maxi finished taping the left hand and went on to the right. Kenny, like most boxers, was superstitious. He had to have things done in order.

'Tick tock, 'alf an hour goes by an' they're still at it!' Maxi continued his story. 'I mean, I thought it was down to a swift Donald then back to the jollies downstairs. So I stick a fag in me mouth, lean out round the edge of the bed . . . and there they are, goin' for the cup. So I taps the bird on the arse an' says . . . all polite like . . . 'Scuse me.' Maxi could hardly speak he was laughing so hard. ' 'Scuse me . . . got a light?'

Kenny was laughing, so was Eddie.

'You should've seen her face. She can't believe it. An' there's me, lookin' as innocent as baby Jesus!'

In Charlie Locke's changing room, Charlie was with his manager and trainer and his wife, Margaret. He had his foot up on a bench. Margaret slipped off her wedding ring and passed it to Charlie. He carefully tied it in the lace of one of his boots, for luck.

Dave Dury, Mel and two or three close friends looked in briefly to give their good wishes.

Kenny was warming up, working on his neck muscles, when the Fox mob came pouring in. They surrounded him, the men shaking his taped fists, the women giving him kisses. Kenny noticed

Bette and looked at her outfit in surprise.

'This is Bette, Kenny. I told you about her,' said Joey.

'I read the cards on you today,' Bette said. 'You're going to win.'

Kenny laughed. 'Thanks.'

'Any special round?' Maxi asked.

'Five. Round five.'

'If she says five you better believe it, Kenny,' Vin said ruefully and everyone laughed.

The hall was packed as the Fox family filed in to take their seats in the front row, Billy leading the way. Dave Dury was already in his seat also in the front, at right angles to them, when he saw Joey come in at the end of the file. He took a wad of money from his pocket and held it up to show Joey. Billy noticed the pantomime and leaned back to have a word with Ray.

'What's that all about?'

'Joey's got a bet on.'

'With that poisoned dog?'

'You know him?'

'I knew his old man, Alf Dury. He was another tripehound. This bet – how much?'

'I'm not sure.'

Ray was lying and Billy knew it. 'How much?' he asked again.

'Ask Joey.'

Billy left his seat and walked over to speak to Joey. Joey said something and Billy's expression made it clear what he thought of him.

The undercard had some tasty fights on it but everyone was waiting for the main event, the big one. The noisy arena hushed as the bell rang for the preliminaries. The Master of Ceremonies introduced the fight in classic fashion.

'Gentlemen, please!' he began. The crowd quietened. 'My Lords, Ladies and Gentlemen . . . this is a ten round, welterweight contest at three minutes each round . . .'

Kenny was dancing in his corner, keeping warm. Charlie Locke was being massaged by his trainer. They stood in turn, arms raised, to acknowledge the cheers from the packed hall when the MC introduced them.

The two fighters met in the centre of the ring for the referee's instructions. Charlie Locke started to eyeball Kenny, who ignored him. They went back to their corners. Waiting for the bell, Charlie Locke crossed himself. Eddie slipped Kenny's gumshield into his mouth.

'Remember, *box* him Kenny. Take your time . . . settle. He's bang on the weight, he could be a bit dehydrated. He ain't goin' to last,' added Maxi quickly.

'So watch him for a fast start,' was Eddie's last bit of advice before the bell went for Round One.

The fight quickly developed a pattern, Charlie's aggression and power against Kenny's boxing skills. Charlie came tearing into Kenny from the first bell, roughing him up. He tried everything he knew to throw Kenny's balance and control. From early on his head came in hard in the clashes. Kenny's crowd made sure the ref knew in no uncertain terms, but Charlie continued his tactics. The referee cautioned Charlie, just before the first round ended, for careless use of his head.

In the second round Charlie put Kenny down with a wicked right. Kenny got up, too early, at a count of six. Eddie wasn't pleased and shouted into the ring to let Kenny know. Nan, in her front row seat, winced and looked anxious but Kenny didn't seem badly hurt and finished the round getting back in control.

In the third round Charlie dropped Kenny again. The Fox family screamed at Kenny to get up, the women leading the shouting. But this time Eddie signalled him to stay down. Kenny nodded to his corner that he was all right and waited for a count of nine before he got up. At the end of the round Eddie got him in the corner and gave him a real earful.

Charlie kept up the onslaught in Round Four. Suddenly there was a cut over Kenny's left eye. It looked bad, there was quite a bit of blood. Charlie attacked in flurries of action, forcing Kenny back. Billy shouted for the referee to watch Charlie's nut going in. Dave Dury reckoned it was all over and indicated his feeling to Joey by giving him a thumbs down for Kenny as the round ended.

Back in the corner, Maxi worked expertly on the cut. It wasn't as bad as it looked. The referee came over to have a look, but Eddie spoke to him and he was satisfied. Kenny could continue.

The bell sounded for Round Five. Charlie was after the cut

eye. His head came in again, hard. The referee warned him, more seriously this time, and some of the crowd began to boo Charlie, but he kept up the attack. Suddenly Kenny caught Charlie, hard, as he came in. Then Kenny caught him again – and a third time. For the first time, Charlie started to go backwards. The Fox family were on their feet, going wild. Charlie was all over the place, his legs were going. Eddie and Maxi urged Kenny on. Charlie tried to grab Kenny and hold on but the referee forced him to break and fight. Kenny let go a terrific left hook to Charlie's temple. Charlie's head snapped back, his jaw sagged open and the gumshield went flying as he crashed to the canvas. No one watching had the slightest thought that Charlie Locke would get up after that punch.

The referee sent Kenny to a neutral corner and stood over Charlie to go through the formal ritual of counting him out.

The Fox mob went wild. Ray, Vin and Joey jumped into the ring. Eddie and Maxi tried to get them to return to their seats. The referee raised Kenny's arm. Joey picked Kenny up as the MC tried to make the winning announcement.

'Gentlemen, please . . .' the MC began. 'In one minute fifty seconds of the fifth round, the winner by a knockout and new Southern Welterweight Champion – Kenny Fox!'

Even in the confusion in the ring Kenny could see that Charlie Locke was still unconscious, his seconds trying to revive him. Joey went over to the edge of the ring to give the finger to Dave Dury as he was leaving with Mel, his face grim. Eddie and Kenny moved to Charlie's corner to see if he was all right. The doctor climbed into the ring and knelt beside Charlie who was still clean out. Margaret, Charlie's wife, stood by white-faced as the doctor tried to revive him. Charlie looked very pale but slowly regained consciousness.

Back in the dressing room, conflicting strands of conversation barraged round Kenny's head as Maxi cut the tape from his hands. First, there were the congratulations. Billy and Joey were telling him what a great fight it had been, and Eddie was concerned to get the doctor to look at Kenny's cut eye. There was great laughter that Bette's prediction for round five had been true. Amid comments about Charlie's knockdown, the women had noticed his wife's pale face and felt sorry for her. Nan, who probably more than the others could put herself in Margaret's place, thought she'd looked physically ill. With all this going on around him, Kenny had a strange feeling about the outcome of the fight. He couldn't understand why he didn't feel elated, like his family. After all, he'd done his job well, hadn't he?

When Eddie finally got the doctor he turned to Billy. 'We'll see you back at the house, eh?'

'Sure, sure, Eddie.' Billy understood. 'Come on, you lot . . . out.'

'I'll stay, Billy,' said Nan, looking anxiously at the eye.

Billy called over his shoulder, the last to leave, 'Don't be too long. We've got a lot of celebrating to do!'

'That'll need a couple of stitches,' the doctor said. 'I'll come back when he's stopped sweating.'

Nan put her arm round Kenny as the doctor left. Maxi went with him and had a word with the face outside.

'Don't let anyone else in, Stan.'

Stan nodded and Maxi closed the door.

In Ray's car going home the mood was ecstatic. Ray drove, Billy next to him. Joey, Bette and Connie were in the back. All the men were smoking big cigars. Bette, being Bette, smoked one too. Billy was uncorking a bottle of champagne Ray had brought. Joey started to sing.

'Kenny Fox, Kenny Fox, watch that little bastard box!'

The others joined in.

'Kenny Fox, Kenny Fox, watch that little bastard box! Kenny Fox . . .'

The shampoo cork popped, the wine spurting all over the interior of the car. Bette squealed as it sprayed over her. Ray powered the big car through South London as the bottle was passed round.

Kenny had his eye stitched and plastered when he and Nan, with Eddie and Maxi, left the dressing room to go home. They were walking towards the exit when two ambulance men hurried past with a stretcher on wheels. Kenny tried to follow but Eddie held him back.

'Leave it, Kenny.'

'But I've got to—'

'Leave it. You can't do anything.'

'He'll be fine,' Maxi tried to help

'How do you know?' Kenny flared. 'How the hell do you

know?' Again, Kenny went to move up the corridor. Once more, Eddie prevented him.

'Kenny, please, don't go up there.'

'I've got to, Eddie!' Kenny pulled away.

'Don't, Kenny,' Nan pleaded.

'I can't just walk away,' Kenny said. He went quickly up the corridor after the ambulance men, clutching his boxing bag.

In Charlie's changing room the doctor and the ambulance men were carefully lifting him on to the stretcher. He was unconscious again and deadly pale. They wrapped him in red blankets. Margaret was holding on to Charlie's trainer, crying quietly. The men pushed the loaded stretcher out into the corridor.

Kenny stood to one side to let the stretcher out. Eddie had a quick mumbled word with Charlie's manager. Kenny was too stunned to say anything. He was almost crying as the stretcher was rushed down the dingy corridor.

TEN

KENNY walked across Clapham Common in the early morning, hollow-eyed from lack of sleep. His face was unshaven, the bruises coming out on it. He didn't seem to be walking anywhere, just walking. He tried hard not to remember the dreams he'd been having, awful surrealist nightmares of corruption and death. He shivered, but from the cold inside.

Kenny started to jog as though out on early morning training. The jog became a run as he tried to put it all out of his mind, to force the pain away. He started sprinting, eyes tightly shut, running blind. He ran and ran. In his head he saw, as in very slow motion, the sickening punch that knocked Charlie Locke down He saw the perfection of the left hook landing on the temple, the sag of the face and jaw and the spray of sweat as the gumshield flew out, the angle of the falling body as it crashed to the canvas.

Kenny ran and ran and then he fell. He lay face down on the Common, not moving. Then he rolled over on to his back and stared up at the early morning spring sky and slowly came back to life.

The strange, inquisitive face of an old greyhound bitch pushed itself into Kenny's square of sky. Kenny didn't move, then he saw the face of Jacko peering down at him. Jacko was a harmless old man he'd often seen exercising two geriatric greyhounds while he was doing his early morning runs.

'Saw you fall. You all right, son?'

'Hello, Jacko.' Kenny sat up, and the funny old man helped him to his feet.

'Where's the sambo?'

'What?'

'You run with . . . see you most mornings . . . big black feller?'

'I'm not trainin' this mornin', Jacko.'

'Oh. Saw you runnin' . . . thought you was.'

'Not this mornin'.'

Kenny started to walk away. Jacko followed, the greyhounds at his heel. 'What you runnin' for then?'

'Just runnin'.'

Kenny quickened his pace across the Common. 'See yer, Jacko.'

'Most mornin's,' Jacko said, falling behind. He bent down and started to thread a long piece of string through the collar of one of his greyhounds.

Billy was up early, washed and shaved, and in the kitchen putting on the kettle for some tea. He stopped, tea caddy in his hand, when he saw the back door was slightly open. He quietly went back upstairs, then listened for a moment outside Kenny's door. He opened the door and saw Kenny's empty bed.

A few minutes later, Billy was out in his car looking for him. He drove along the Common and stopped when he saw Jacko and his dogs. He called twice before the old boy heard him. When he caught up with him, Jacko pointed to his lapel.

'Where's yer flower, Billy?'

'Have you seen Kenny?'

'Fell over.'

'Kenny?'

'Runnin' . . . alone . . . runnin' fast,' Jacko explained. 'Tripped, fell over. Thought 'e was hurt, asked 'im, 'e wasn't. Just runnin', 'e said, not trainin', just runnin'.'

'When, Jacko?'

'This mornin'.'

'Yes but when – how long ago?' Billy asked impatiently.

'Not long.'

'Which way did he go?'

Jacko pointed a direction.

'Thanks, Jacko.'

'If I see 'im again, I'll tell 'im yer lookin' fer 'im, Billy.'

'Good old boy,' Billy said. He walked back to his car, got in and drove off across the Common road.

Kenny ran for a bus as it pulled away from the stop and gathered speed. He hurled himself on it, helped by the conductor. He slumped down on a bench seat, getting his breath back.

'Where to, John?' The conductor was a good-looking West Indian with a thick South London accent.

'King's College.'

'Hospital?'

Kenny nodded. The conductor took his money and gave him a

ticket. He took a long look at Kenny's bruised face.

'Who give yer that little lot?'

Kenny touched his face with the tips of his fingers. 'Looks worse than it is.'

The conductor looked hard at him.

'Don't I know you? Know yer face. Seen yer face, somewhere recent. In the paper, right?'

Kenny was getting edgy; he wanted to be left alone, but the conductor's face lit up as he remembered:

'Ain't you a boxer? Course – the face, you're that boxer.'

The bus slowed to turn a corner, and Kenny got up suddenly and jumped off, leaving the conductor standing on the platform, calling the name he'd just remembered. 'Fox . . . Kenny Fox!'

Kenny turned his back on the bus and moved away. In his head the sound of the conductor calling his name changed to the MC introducing him to the fight crowd.

'Kenny Fox!' He heard the crowd's roar of approval and it all started again.

Nan saw that Connie looked drawn and nervous when she opened the door. Nan linked arms with her.

'Is he back yet?'

'Billy's still out looking for him.'

'I thought, driving over, maybe he's gone to the hospital?'

'Billy rang,' Connie said. 'He wasn't there.' They walked down the hall.

'Was there any news about Charlie Locke?'

'He's still unconscious.'

The telephone rang, and Connie picked it up quickly, hoping it was Kenny or Billy.

'Hello?'

Nan stood behind her waiting for some sort of news. She watched Connie's face harden.

'Who are you? No, he's not in. No, not this morning, no . . . No . . . because *I said so*. It wouldn't be convenient.' Connie slammed down the receiver.

'Who was it?'

'Who do they think they are?' Connie was very angry. 'Some reporter . . . wanted to come over.'

*

In the hospital waiting room Charlie Locke's manager was slumped in a chair. He'd been smoking for hours. The ashtray on the floor beside him was filled with half-smoked cigarettes. Billy came in and closed the door. Arthur looked shagged, he thought.

'Any news?'

'He's paralysed down one side.'

'Oh Christ . . . I am sorry, Arthur,' Billy mumbled. 'How's his wife taking it?'

'Pretty bad. Bob run her home to see the kid's all right.'

'Is there anything we can do?'

'Wish there was.'

'No sign of Kenny?'

Arthur shook his head. 'He took it bad?'

'I've never seen 'im like that before . . .'

'He's a sensible lad, Billy. Don't you fret, he'll be all right.'

'I'm more worried about your boy than mine,' Billy said sadly.

'He had trouble making the weight. The way he folded up, he must've been dehydrated.' Arthur sounded exhausted.

Billy tried to be positive. 'Remember Bobby Neill when Spinsky knocked him out, that happened to him, and look at him now, top man.'

'Yeah, of course . . . you're right. But he never fought again,' Arthur said ruefully. 'All that talent . . . one punch.'

'That one punch . . . it could bugger both of them!' Billy said.

A flashy American car crept slowly down the road towards Joey's flat. Mel, Dave Dury's minder, checked the number. He passed Joey's cab, which was parked a little way from the house. He braked, looked the cab over and moved on. When he found the house he pulled the big car into a parking space.

Joey came out just as Mel was parking.

'Oi . . . taxi driver.'

'You talkin' to me?' Joey stopped and turned.

'I don't see no one else.'

Joey sensed trouble and sized Mel up. He was a big bastard, no doubt about that.

'What can I do for you, feller?' Joey said tightly.

'Don't get tense.' Mel smiled.

'I'm in a hurry.'

Mel took out the grand in tenners. There were two fat bundles with the bank wrappers still round them.

'Dave asked me to drop this over, with his compliments.'

Joey looked at the money. 'No thanks,' he said. He turned to his cab to unlock it.

'What d'yer mean?'

'What I said.'

'It's a grand!'

'I don't want it.'

'You won it.' Mel held out the money.

'I don't *want* it.'

'It's a bet.'

'Look, pal, do us both a favour, leave it, eh?'

'Dave always pays what's due,' Mel said stolidly.

'He's a gentleman,' Joey said sarcastically.

Mel tried to stuff the money in the front of Joey's jacket. 'One grand . . . delivered!'

'Rub off!' Joey pulled away angrily.

'You're tryin' me!' Mel threatened.

Joey pointed to Mel's car. 'Why don't you get back in that chrome coffin and take that with you?'

'Dave wouldn't appreciate that.'

'I don't give two shits.'

Joey unlocked his cab. Mel put his hand on the door, stopping Joey from getting in. 'Don't make me mistreat you.'

Joey shrugged, he could see Mel was looking for trouble. He held his hand out for the money.

Mel smiled. 'Tell your brother it was a lucky punch . . . for *you.*'

Mel dumped the money in Joey's hand and let go of the taxi door. Joey got in, started up the engine. Mel walked back to his car. When he was almost there, Joey pulled his cab out fast and accelerated up to Mel. He called out of the window.

'Oi . . . mouth!' Joey tossed the money on top of the Yank car. It slid off the roof and dropped in the gutter at Mel's feet, into a puddle. Mel stooped down to retrieve it as Joey drove off fast. He picked the money out of the dirty water, and shook it dry, taking care not to get his suit wet. He threw the bundles of notes on to the passenger seat.

'A f . . . f . . . funny man!' he said to himself. When he got very cross it brought on a childhood stutter.

*

Kenny had made his way to the hospital sometime before but hadn't been able to force himself to go in. It had rained while he stood looking through the railings, unsure. His clothes were still wet but he wandered inside the building and found the ward area he was looking for. As he approached a side room he saw a nurse leaving. He waited for her to go, then went to the door and looked in.

Charlie Locke was wired up to a machine that monitored his heart-beat, pulse and blood pressure. He was still unconscious, with a breathing tube in his mouth like an obscene child's dummy. Kenny slipped into the room and just stood, staring at Charlie. He remembered the words they'd exchanged at the weigh-in.

'I've already beat you twice,' Charlie had said.

'Long time ago, Charlie. We was amateurs. You're an old man now.'

Charlie looked like an old man now, all right, with all the colour drained from his face, and his eyes closed. It looked like a death mask.

A voice intruded on Kenny's thoughts, and he had to force himself back into the present.

'Who are you?' the nurse asked. 'What are you doing in here?'

'I came to see . . .' His voice tailed off.

'Would you please leave?' Her voice was crisp and efficient.

'How . . . how is he?'

'I'll have to call the sister if you don't.' She waited a moment. 'Are you the other one? The other boxer?'

'Yes.'

'There's another gentleman in the waiting room.' She sounded more sympathetic as she eased Kenny out of the room. 'He's been here all night. Why don't you talk to him?'

The waiting room was empty when Kenny went in. He saw the crumpled cigarette packets Arthur Graham had left, next to the overflowing ashtray. He had his back to the door when he heard someone come in behind him – Charlie Locke's wife. She looked completely exhausted, her face pale and her eyes red from crying. They stood watching each other for a long time before Margaret spoke in a quiet, strained voice.

'He's only twenty-six,' she said.

Kenny couldn't find any words.

'We've only been married two years.'

Kenny dropped his head, he couldn't bear to look at her.

'He was always joking. No one could ever hurt him . . . not him . . . no one.'

Arthur Graham had gone out for cigarettes. When he came back he saw Kenny and Margaret through the window of the waiting room. He watched them talking, then went to phone Billy.

'I've never understood why . . .' Margaret was saying. 'What makes Charlie, you, all the others want to fight. What is it, inside, makes you do it, enjoy it . . . *need* it? Charlie's not a violent man. I suppose that sounds silly?'

'No, it doesn't,' Kenny said quietly.

'He's so gentle with me and the baby.' She smiled briefly. 'When she was born he wouldn't hold her in case he hurt her.'

'When you're in the ring you change,' Kenny tried to explain. 'You're something else, someone else. You're so wound up – crowd screamin', sweat pourin' off – all you want to do is catch him, again . . . again!' Kenny was lost in his explanation, he didn't realise what he was saying. He had the fight crowd in his ears again. 'Hurt him, you can feel it when you hurt him . . . all you want to do is to hurt him bad—' Kenny stopped suddenly. He looked at Margaret, her eyes brimming with tears.

'Christ! I'm sorry . . .'

Margaret hurriedly brushed the tears away as they spilled down.

'I'm sorry. I didn't think what I . . .' Kenny didn't know what to do.

'It's all right.' Margaret, embarrassed, tried to get hold of herself.

Kenny wanted to put his arms round her to comfort her but he couldn't move.

'You shouldn't have come,' Margaret said.

'Charlie would have,' he said simply.

Arthur Graham joined them in the waiting room, and was just lighting a cigarette for Margaret when the nurse came in.

'Mrs Locke.'

Margaret looked up at the nurse, her face full of apprehension.

'Doctor Fleming would like to see you in Sister's office.' The nurse gave her a professional smile of assurance. Margaret stubbed out her newly lit cigarette.

'I'll come with you,' said Arthur.

As they left, Arthur turned back to Kenny. 'Take it easy, son.'

Then they walked out with the nurse, and Kenny was alone. He started to shiver; he couldn't stop himself remembering. The shiver became a shake. Now he heard the crowd roaring and screaming as Charlie went down. Kenny's whole body was shaking.

ELEVEN

DAVE Dury was lying naked, face down on a sun bed. His eyes were hidden by protective glasses. The room was full of exercising gear with a rowing machine, bicycle, abdominal board, bench press machine and dumb-bells. There was a large mirror on one wall, a huge photo blow-up of Steve Reeves flexing his muscles on another. Soft music oozed from an expensive cassette player within easy reach of the sunbed. After a knock on the door, a voice came from outside the room.

'Mel,' it said.

'Take yer shoes off,' Dury ordered.

Mel walked in shoeless. He had a hole in the heel of one sock and he carried the thousand pounds.

Dury saw the money. 'Couldn't you find 'im?'

'No bother,' said Mel.

'Well?'

'He don't want it, wouldn't take it. Th . . . th . . . threw it in the gutter.'

'Oh dear.' Dury's reaction was deceptively mild.

'He's a lump!' Mel said viciously.

'Where is he now?'

'He went off in his hack.'

'Find 'im,' Dury ordered tersely.

'He's a maggot, don't let 'im bother you, Dave. You're a grand to the good.'

Dury wasn't looking for advice. 'I said *find him.*'

Mel started to leave with the money. Dury pointed to it.

'Leave that.'

'But you said—'

'*You* find him . . . *I'll* deliver the dough.'

As Mel turned to go, Dury saw the spud in his sock heel.

'Don't you have no pride in your personal appearance?' he asked wearily.

Kenny was slumped in a chair when Billy, Connie and Nan came in.

'Arthur phoned us,' Billy explained.

'We were worried, Kenny,' said Connie.

Nan put her arms round him. 'You're wet . . . your jacket's soaked.'

'Got caught in the rain.'

Billy started to take off the jacket.

'It's all right, Pop. I'm *all right*. Just . . . just leave me be!' Kenny flared.

Billy put the jacket back patiently. 'Where's Arthur?'

'Gone with Charlie's wife to see a doctor.' Kenny looked very concerned.

'Maybe it's good news?' Connie said gently.

'I saw him – Charlie. He's in a side room, all wired up to a machine, this thing in his mouth. He looked so . . . *so old.*'

Nan gave him a little hug. 'There's nothing you can do here, love.'

'I'm stayin',' Kenny said firmly, and pulled away. 'If that's what you've come for, you're wasting your time.'

'Be sensible, son,' Billy said. 'Be *fair . . . to her*, Charlie's missus. She won't want you hangin' round now, will she?'

Kenny hardly noticed what Billy was saying.

'They've only been married two years,' Kenny said to Nan.

It was obviously going to be difficult to get him to leave. Through the window of the room Billy saw Arthur, beckoning. Making an excuse about getting some coffee, Billy left the others. Arthur explained that the doctors had decided to operate on Charlie, whose condition was dangerous. Between them, they cooked up a scheme to get Kenny away from the hospital. It meant laying it on a bit thick, but Arthur agreed it was best to get Kenny home. According to plan, Billy went off for coffee and Arthur walked in to the waiting room.

'Didn't Billy come?' Arthur asked Connie innocently.

'He's gone to get some coffee.'

'What's happening?' Kenny asked Arthur.

'She's in with him now,' Arthur lied.

Kenny brightened. 'Has he come round?'

'Not yet but they're hopeful, that's why they want her in there. Look, Kenny, I don't want to sound snide, but I think it's best all round if you went home. It's upset her seeing you. Nothing you've said or anything, it's just she's got enough to cope with at the moment.'

Kenny clenched his left fist and held it out. 'I'd cut it off if I thought it'd help!'

Arthur put an arm round Kenny, and slowly walked him to the door. Connie and Nan followed.

'I know, son. I know how you must be feeling.'

Billy arrived with two plastic cups of coffee just as they were leaving. He turned and walked with them, still carrying the coffee.

Billy's car drew up to the house. As they all got out a reporter came up to them. He was about thirty, with long hair and a beard, scruffily dressed.

'Excuse me, my name is Colin Street. I phoned earlier.'

Connie turned to Billy. 'That reporter.'

'Was it you I spoke to?' Street asked Connie. 'I didn't explain very well—'

'My wife told you to stay away,' Billy said belligerently.

'Not exactly—' Street began.

'You go in,' Billy told Connie. 'I'll sort this.'

They moved towards the front door of the house, but Street was anxious to talk to Kenny.

'You've been to the hospital?'

Kenny pushed past him, but Street was insistent, and tried to follow.

'I've heard they're going to operate on Charlie Locke?'

Kenny stopped dead in his tracks. 'Operate?'

Billy quickly moved between Kenny and the reporter. 'On yer bike, whiskers!' he threatened.

'Who told you that?' asked Kenny.

'You didn't know?'

Billy shoved him. 'Out of it!'

Street wasn't deterred by Billy's show of aggression. Kenny turned to Billy. 'Is it true, Pop?'

'I thought you'd have been told,' Street said.

'He's just givin' you a gee up, son.' Billy looked at Street. 'You shut your lyin' mouth.'

'All I want is five minutes with Kenny. I know the situation must be stressful but—'

'You scruffy slag!' Billy exploded. 'You don't give a toss about Kenny *or* Charlie. All the same you lot are, sliming around decent people, twistin' what they do say, makin' up what they *don't* say!'

The front door of the house opened, and Eddie appeared with Vin and Joey.

'What's up, Billy?' Eddie asked.

'This lard arse reporter—'

Vin stepped forward. 'I think you'd better get lost,' he said.

Street, still not phased, spoke directly to Billy. 'I write the truth as I see it, Mr Fox. I don't make it up, I don't need to. You think you're protecting Kenny by lying to him – that's good copy.'

Billy wasn't able to control himself any longer. He hooked Street, who went down on the ground.

Vin grabbed Billy. 'No! Pop!'

Then Eddie took charge while Billy struggled with Vin to get at Street again.

'Let me deal with this,' Eddie said firmly.

Street picked himself up, his nose bleeding. He wiped the blood away on the back of his hand and pointed back to his car. A photographer was leaning on it to steady a long telephoto lens. He was blitz-clicking away.

'Thanks very much,' Street said. 'If you want it this way—'

Joey was after the photographer before Eddie could stop him, but the smudge man calmly crashed off a couple of shots of Joey charging at him, then jumped in the car and quickly locked all the doors. Joey was left outside, grimacing as he tried to get in. The photographer crouched in the back seat, shooting more pictures of Joey's furious face.

Eddie ran up to Joey, who had started rocking the car violently. 'What's the matter with you, Joey?'

'I want that bleedin' camera!'

'You're only making it worse,' Eddie pulled him away. 'For *Kenny*!'

This gave Joey something to think about and he calmed down. Eddie finally persuaded them all to go inside. Vin was still having a hard time calming Billy, who had to have his last word with Street.

'You stay away from my house!' he was shouting as Vin led him inside.

Eddie walked back with Street, whose nose was still bleeding. 'Look, I'm sorry about that. It's been a rough morning.'

'So that's King Billy,' Street said ruefully.

'He isn't usually like that. What did you say to him?'

From their front room, the Fox family watched as Eddie and Street got back to the press car. The photographer cautiously got out, leaving his camera safely on the back seat.

'You shouldn't have hit him, Billy,' said Connie. But Billy was unrepentent.

They watched as Eddie shook hands with Street and the photographer.

'Looks like Eddie's squared him,' Vin said.

Street and the photographer got in the car and drove off, and Eddie walked slowly back to the house. The front door slammed and he came in looking very stern. He stood in the doorway looking at Billy and Joey with recrimination, but saying nothing.

They were all having a cup of tea in Billy's living room when Nan came downstairs. She had been trying to talk to Kenny, who was in his bedroom, not saying anything. Nan was trying hard not to cry.

'Give it a couple of days, Nan,' said Eddie. He stood up to give her a little comforting hug. 'I'll go and have a word.' Eddie made his way slowly and thoughtfully up the stairs.

In Kenny's room everything was as tidy as ever. Kenny was sitting, hunched up, on the side of the bed. He looked up.

'Are you going to lie as well?'

'Have I ever lied to you, Kenny?'

'I don't know. Have you?'

'That's a shitty thing to say.'

'I'm tired, Eddie.'

'I thought I knew you.' Kenny looked surprised but Eddie went on. 'Thought you had a bit more bottle than this, a bit more consideration. Who are you feeling sorry for, Kenny, except yourself?'

'Why didn't they tell me about the operation?' Kenny defended himself. 'All that bullshit at the hospital. Everything's goin' to be all right, Kenny . . . he's comin' round, Kenny . . . we know how you're feelin', Kenny!'

'How do you think *they're* feeling?' Eddie countered. 'Your Mum, Dad, Vinnie, Joey? You think it's easy for them, seeing you in this state? Billy's aged ten years this morning. He was out looking for you at seven o'clock.'

'I went for a walk,' Kenny said sullenly.

'You could've left a note . . . you could've telephoned from the hospital.'

'I didn't 'ave to, did I?' Kenny said sourly. 'Billy 'ad Arthur Graham well cautioned.'

'What did you expect him to do – just sit and wait for you to make up your mind to come home? The state you was in, that could've been never.'

'What was I goin' to do, top meself?' Kenny said mockingly.

'Maybe—'

'Don't be bloody daft!'

'It goes through your mind, son. You can laugh, but it goes through your mind, however much you don't want to think about it. Ask Nan.'

'Did she say that?'

'She didn't have to.'

Kenny dropped his head.

It was unusually quiet in the taxi driver's cafe. Joey and Griff were sitting together over a cup of tea, talking about Charlie Locke.

'They're goin' to ring Billy from the hospital as soon as the operation's over.'

'I s'pose it could be well into tomorrer before the poor sod comes round. I mean after an operation like that . . . it's all goin' to take time.'

'Yeah.'

'I wouldn't fancy 'em pokin' round in my loaf,' Griff said, pointing. 'Would you?'

Joey smiled. 'All they'd find up there is ten-year-old jokes and about five thousand street names.' He checked his watch. 'I better be gettin' back. I just needed five minutes away from it all.'

Griff finished his cuppa and came after him. Outside, Griff was the first to spot Joey's cab.

'Jesus, Joey . . . look!'

The back of the taxi was literally papered with one pound notes. They were on the windows, spread on the back seat, on the floor, stuffed in the ashtrays. Joey opened the back door and half a dozen notes blew on to the pavement. Griff hurriedly gathered them up while Joey stood looking inside.

'Bloody 'ell!' Griff said.

Dave Dury's maroon Corniche, with Mel at the wheel, hissed to a stop beside them. The electric window wound down and Dury leaned out.

'I'm a good loser, taxi driver.'

Then the window whined up as the car moved away almost noiselessly. Joey and Griff just stood there.

'I've seen some things in my time . . .' Griff was saying when Joey noticed his front tyre. He slowly walked round the cab. All the tyres were flat.

'He's done yer tyres, Joey!' Griff kneeled down to inspect one. There was a deep knife cut in it.

'The shit'ead!' Griff exclaimed.

Joey just stood looking at his vandalised cab.

The operation was over. Charlie Locke was in the post-op intensive care unit, wired to a battery of machines. A nurse was checking the readings, noting them on a clip board. Margaret and Arthur, wearing face masks and surgical gowns, stood as close to Charlie as they were allowed. Margaret was holding a photograph. She tried to speak through the mask.

' 'Scuse me.'

The nurse looked up from her clipboard.

'Could I . . . could I leave this?' Margaret held out the photograph. 'For when he wakes up.'

'Of course.' The nurse smiled. She made a show of propping it up, so that it could easily be seen from the bed. The photograph was of Margaret and their year-old baby. The nurse went back to her monitoring and Margaret and Arthur turned to leave.

Colin Street was lurking in the corridor as they came out. He'd been watching them before, waiting for the right moment to make his approach. Now he came up as they walked slowly down the corridor.

Joey stood in the phone box, listening to the number ringing and looking at the cab parked outside with four, brand new tyres. He'd called a taxi breakdown truck and got the job done in an hour.

'Hello,' Connie said at the other end.

'It's Joey.' He told Connie most of the story after finding there was no news yet about Charlie Locke. 'And while I'm up 'ere I'll pop round to see Bette. I won't be long, but if you get any news here's her number.'

At Bette's house Joey rang the bell several times and was about to go back to his cab when the door opened. She was barefoot, dressed in a kaftan, and stoned.

'Joey?' she asked hazily.

He could see she was blitzed. 'You've been licking too many stamps.'

'I'm very . . . okie dokie.' She stumbled inside.

Joey followed her into a room with a monster television set. A VCR machine was linked to it, playing back an old Bette Davis movie. The room was dark and stank of dope. As Joey's eyes adjusted to the lack of light he made out two figures lying on cushions, passing a twenty-eight skinner between them. Bette gave a mock introduction.

'This . . . this is Joey.' She giggled. 'Foxy Joey. I told you about him.'

Joey could see the figures more clearly. One was a beautiful black chick, the other a hard-faced white girl. They looked like models and they both ignored him.

'I come round to tell you about Kenny.' Joey felt uncomfortable. 'I thought you'd want to know.'

'Kenny?' Bette was really out of it. '*Kenny* Kenny?'

He didn't like Bette like this. He saw the girls put their arms round each other and kiss. For a moment he couldn't believe it, they were kissing like lovers.

'How is he?' Bette asked at last.

'W . . . what?' Joey was watching the girls.

'You came round to tell me about Kenny?'

Joey suddenly turned and walked out of the room.

'Joey?' Bette called after him.

Joey moved quickly towards the door to get out of the house as soon as he could.

'Joey!' Bette called again. She had stumbled to the door of the television room and stood watching him. Joey stopped and turned to face her.

'You rubbish . . .' He couldn't find the right words. 'You . . . dirty trash!'

As he snatched the front door open he heard stoned laughter coming from the television room. Bette started to giggle.

TWELVE

PHIL stopped Anna's car outside Billy's house. He'd borrowed the car after Anna had shown him the late afternoon papers, headlining the story of Charlie Locke's condition. It was the first he'd heard about it and he knew he had to get home as soon as possible. The hall light came on seconds after he had rung the bell, and Connie's face brightened when she saw him.

'There's something wrong with the phone,' Phil said. 'I tried to call several times.'

Connie put her finger to her lips. 'Nan's asleep in the front room,' she whispered.

Phil wasn't sure how Billy would react on seeing him. 'Hello, Pop,' he said.

There was a moment of uncertainty between them, but Billy saw the absurdity of a family quarrel at this time. 'Why didn't you let us know you were coming?' he said, and Phil relaxed.

'I tried to, couldn't get through.' They went into the living room. 'Where's Kenny?'

'Asleep,' Connie said quietly.

'How is he?'

'You should've seen him last night. He *was* in a state . . .' Billy didn't intend this as a reproof but Phil looked away.

'I ain't sniping at you, son,' Billy said quickly. 'You had your reasons for not coming.'

'We told Kenny you was sick,' Joey said.

'Why?'

'So as not to hurt him,' Billy said.

'You hurt him more by lying to him – can't you see that?' Phil paused. 'Now I'm going to have to lie to him as well.'

'We was coverin' up fer you in the first place,' Joey said aggressively.

'Why? I didn't ask you to. What was so bad about the truth?'

Unable to bear them arguing, Connie intervened. 'What's done's done . . . no one can change it. I don't think I could take you three rowing tonight.' She changed the subject abruptly. 'Are you hungry, Phil?'

*

Colin Street was lurking in the hospital, trying to find the latest news on Charlie Locke. He had been working on the nurse and approached her in the corridor.

'I could lose my job,' she said nervously, looking over her shoulder.

'Who'd know?'

'No—' She was undecided.

'One telephone call,' Street insisted.

'I've got to go.'

She started to walk away, but Street, persistent as ever, followed and held out a card.

'Here's my home and office number. If you change your mind . . .'

'I won't.'

'You might. Think about it.' He forced the card on her. 'It's the easiest money you'll ever earn.'

Phil and Joey got back late to Joey's flat. They were both tired out.

'We can two up in the feather or there's the sofa?' Joey offered.

Phil pointed to the sofa. 'We're old friends.'

' 'Ere, bruv, do you know anything about lesbians?' Joey went through into his bedroom and talked to Phil through the open door. 'You know . . . Two nuns bought a bunch of bananas, found a straight one and said, "We'll have to eat this"!'

'Why, are you thinking of taking the veil?' Phil started undressing.

In the hospital corridor the nurse, hesitant and furtive, headed for the public telephone, and dialled the number on Colin Street's card.

It was not much after dawn, grey light seeping through the windows, when Billy tiptoed down the hall. He was the first up as always. He stopped at the door of the front room, opened it very quietly and peeped in. Nan was fast asleep on the sofa. Billy shut the door and was about to walk down the hall when he saw someone on the porch through the frosted glass windows.

Arthur Graham was standing there, about to ring the bell.

'Arthur . . . thought you was the post,' he said, surprised.

Arthur stood, not quite knowing what to do with himself. His face was grey, his voice flat and brittle.

'He's dead, Billy,' he said.

Since Kenny heard the news that morning he stayed locked in his bedroom. They all tried to get him out, tried to make him talk, but without success. When Phil and Joey arrived they had another go. Billy spoke through the closed door.

'Kenny, Phil's here. He wants to talk to you. Did you hear me?' They all knew Phil had a way with Kenny, like no one else in the family.

Phil pushed close to the door.

'Kenny? Kenny?'

Phil tried to sound very casual. He slipped back into the South London vernacular he was raised on. 'Got a back like a bleedin' washboard,' he said. 'Kipped on Joey's sofa . . . I don't know what he's been doin' on it, springs are shot, dirty devil.'

Phil thought he heard Kenny move inside the room.

'My bird, Anna, wanted to meet you. You'd like her, so would Nan . . . a bit pound note, but nice.'

Phil heard Kenny move up close to the door. He sensed he was getting through.

'She's only nineteen, right tasty, least I reckon.'

The family had gathered round Phil at the door. He got out his wallet, took out a photograph of Anna.

'Want to see a snap of her? I'll push it under the door, eh?'

Everyone's eyes followed as Phil put the smudge under the door. It stayed there, nothing moved, then the last quarter was slowly pulled into the room.

'What d'you think, Kenny?'

The family waited. Kenny hadn't spoken a word since Billy told him about Charlie's death.

'What's her name again?' Kenny asked through the door.

Billy squeezed Phil's arm. Phil gestured to them all to keep very quiet.

'Anna,' he said. 'Bit like Nan, isn't it?'

There was a long pause.

'Kenny?'

'You missed the fight,' he said.

'I was just as upset as you about that, Kenny.'

'You better now?'

'I'm ticking over . . . still feel a bit wobbly. How're *you* feeling? Bloody awful, I bet?'

'You've heard . . . what's happened?'

'Yeah.'

'He's dead. Charlie's dead. Died this morning, never regained consciousness.'

'They told me, Kenny.'

'I killed him,' Kenny said in a flat voice.

Phil knew he had to be very careful. The others stayed silent, and let Phil talk.

'Lots of things contributed to his death, Kenny. Lots of *different* things . . . he had trouble making the weight. You know what that can mean. It sounds like he just folded up in the fifth, before you knocked him out. Is that right?'

Kenny was silent but Phil knew he was there, behind the door.

'Charlie took a lot of stick, he was that sort of fighter. Remember that one we watched on telly . . . the black boy from Harrow? With the funny name?' Phil paused, hoping Kenny would come up with the name. But Kenny remained silent.

'Charlie nicked that one, but only just. He was dropped twice, remember? He was a catcher, Kenny. You only had to look at his face. He was badly marked, he'd take three to land one. You can't carry on like that and not get hurt . . . hurt bad . . . *inside*. It all mounts up, Kenny, every fight, every time. It could have happened any fight—'

Suddenly Joey butted in, trying to help. 'Why don't you open the door so Phil can talk to you properly?' He meant well but his timing was out.

Phil turned on him. 'Shut up!' he said, his voice very low.

'I only thought . . .'

Phil turned back to the door. 'Kenny?'

There was no reply. Billy took the initiative.

'We'll go downstairs, Phil, leave you to talk to Kenny.' Billy gestured to the others. They all went away making a clatter on the stairs. When they were gone, Phil tried again.

'Kenny? They're all gone now. It's just me and you, Kenny.'

To his surprise he heard Kenny unlock the door. It opened an inch, Kenny peered out.

'I could go a cuppa,' Phil said. 'How about you?'

'Up here?' Kenny half opened the door.

'Wherever you want.'

Kenny nodded. Phil turned and called to Connie over the banisters.

'I'll make a pot,' Connie called up thankfully.

'Give us a shout an' I'll come down for it.'

Kenny opened the door fully but Phil waited to be invited in.

'I'm glad you're here, Phil,' he said.

Downstairs, they were all listening.

'He's got him to open the door,' Vin whispered.

'It's all them psychia-whatever-you-call-it books he reads.' Billy grinned.

The press were having a field day on the Charlie Locke story. It was getting a lot of headlines. Billy's house was bombarded with requests for interviews, by phone and by visiting reporters. They were all turned away. Albert's pub was full of pressmen hanging round looking for local colour. Colin Street stayed on top of the story, having been in first. He followed up with an interview with Charlie's widow and he combed through the photographs his man had taken outside Billy's house, looking for a new angle.

In Charlie's house that night Margaret's sister, Gill, was putting the baby to bed. Downstairs, Margaret poured herself another large scotch. Gill came down and watched her taking a large gulp.

'Why don't you go to bed?'

'I wouldn't be able to sleep,' Margaret choked.

'That isn't going to help,' Gill pointed to the scotch.

'Want to bet?' Margaret downed the drink and went to pour another.

'Let me call the doctor?'

'No!' Margaret shouted. 'No doctors. Bloody quacks . . . they let Charlie *die*.'

An old Westminster pulled up near Billy Fox's house. Four yobbos sat in it, checking the street. They waited. When a light went on in the front room, three of them jumped out. The fourth stayed at the wheel, revving the engine. Connie was alone in the front room when the bricks came smashing through the windows. One narrowly missed her, diamonds of broken glass lodging in her hair. For a few moments, Connie was terrified. When all the windows were done, the three hounds piled into the waiting car. The driver gunned it away, tyres smoking.

Within seconds Ray, Joey, Vin and Phil steamed out of the house. Ray's Jag was parked down the road and they leapt into it, doors slamming. Ray burned the big motor down the street after the Westminster.

Inside, Billy and Nan comforted Connie. Billy held her in his arms, she was still trembling.

Kenny ran into the room to see what was happening, saw the wreckage and shut his eyes as the room began to spin around him. He tried to block everything out, but couldn't. He ran out of the room, out of the house. Nan came after him as he got to his car.

'Where are you going, Kenny?'

'Anywhere! Nowhere!'

'I'll come with you!'

'Go back.' Kenny stopped her from getting in, slammed the car into gear and drove off. Nan was left on the pavement.

The Westminster chopped round a tight corner, the Jag after it. The four Fox brothers got quick glimpses of the car they were chasing as it ducked and dived round the South London back-streets, but the Westminster's driver really knew his stuff. Suddenly, they'd lost it. Ray slammed round another tight corner only to realise it was a dead end. Thirty yards ahead of the speeding car was a high wall. Ray spun the wheel and stood on the brake pedal. He managed to hang on when the big car went into a spin. With a scream of tyres the Jag pulled up side on to the wall, so close that neither Vin nor Joey could open their doors to get out.

Kenny sat in his car and looked at the front of Charlie Locke's house. After a while he got out, walked up and rang the front doorbell. Gill opened the door. She knew Kenny's face from the papers.

'She's gone to bed,' she lied.

'Oh yeah. I didn't think. Will you tell her that—'

'Who is it, Gill?' Margaret came into the hall.

'No one.'

'Who are you talking to?' Margaret staggered to the front door.

'It's me,' Kenny said.

Margaret pushed past her sister. She was quite drunk.

'*You!*'

'I'm . . . I'm sorry. I meant to come earlier but I—'

Margaret began to freak. 'I don't want to see *you.* I don't want to ever – *never ever* see *you* again. Why couldn't it have been you?'

'I think you'd better go,' Gill said quickly to Kenny.

'Why couldn't it have been *you* dead?' Margaret repeated. '*You* instead of Charlie?'

Gill tried to restrain her sister. 'Please go,' she said to Kenny.

'You bastard! You horrible bastard. You killed Charlie . . . you *murdered* my Charlie!'

Kenny backed away while Gill held Margaret in the doorway.

'You *murderer*!' she screamed after him as he turned and ran.

'You bloody bastard *murderer*!' Margaret screamed again.

Kenny scrambled into his car, started it and drove off. He forgot to put on his lights and narrowly missed a car pulling out from a side street. The driver pumped his horn and flashed his lights.

Kenny just drove, as far and as fast as he could.

THIRTEEN

ALAN Haywood played his intro to an empty club. All the lights were out, just a pool spot on piano picked up the tight profile of a very beautiful black chick. Madeline, like all good jazz singers, didn't sing the song, she *was* the song. Her haunting voice brought in Steve, Ray's number one at the club, to listen quietly to the run through. He was a big, good-looking man, as hard as they come. He just sat there and listened while the voice floated through the empty room.

At Billy's house, Ray and Vin did a temporary repair on the windows with hardboard and black polythene sheeting. They cleared most of the glass but bits were still left here and there.

'I'll give Pete Clayton a bell in a minute,' Vin said as he sipped the coffee Connie had brought. 'Get one of his lads over early termorrer to reglaze them.'

'The frames are gone in places,' Ray said.

'Yeah. Might need a chippie too.'

Ray put his arm round Connie's shoulder. 'You okay now, love?'

'Just shook me up a bit.'

'They've got some comin'!' Ray said harshly.

'Pity we didn't get a good look at them,' said Joey.

'We got a good look at that motor.'

'Probably nicked?' Vin suggested.

'No, not the way that slippery bastard was driving,' Ray figured. 'He knew that motor . . . knew exactly what it could do.'

'He certainly pushed it about a bit,' Joey said grudgingly.

The phone rang and Connie went to answer it. No one spoke at the other end.

Vin came out to see who it was. 'It might be Kenny.'

'Kenny? Kenny? Is that you, Kenny?' Connie asked desperately before she slowly replaced the receiver.

'Rang off,' she said.

'Could have bin a wrong number,' said Vin.

'No. Whoever it was put his money in; the pips stopped.' Connie looked at Vin helplessly.

Kenny stepped uncertainly from the call box and walked dully over to his car. An opened bottle of scotch was wedged down beside the passenger seat. Kenny reached for it, unscrewed the top and took a hefty belt. He pulled a pained face as the alcohol hit the back of his throat, then he methodically screwed the top back on and wedged the bottle in its place. He laid his arms round the steering wheel, and dropped his swimming head on them, closing his eyes. He heard Connie's voice calling to him again.

'Kenny, Kenny? Is that you, Kenny?'

He sat up and sucked in a deep breath, trying to get hold of himself. But he couldn't get away from it . . . he heard the sound of breaking glass, bricks smashing through the windows of his house, followed by Margaret's drunken screams.

'Why couldn't it have been *you* dead instead of Charlie . . . You horrible bastard, you killed Charlie . . . you *murdered* my Charlie!'

Kenny started the car. To escape the voices he drove off like a lunatic, crashing the gears.

When Ray got to the club, Steve was on the door.

'Seen anythink of Kenny?'

'Kenny?' Steve was puzzled. 'No, I thought 'e was—'

'Keep yer eyes skinned for 'im, Steve.'

'What's happened?'

'Tell you about it later.' Ray started to go inside.

'There's some filth inside.'

'Who?'

'Alex Tupper, Cullis, and one I don't know. Looks like my dog from behind, all bollocks and back legs. Got a couple of old steamers with 'em.'

Ray smiled. Steve held the door open.

'That bird turned up with Alan,' Steve said.

'What bird?'

'The singer.'

'What's she like?'

'Very choice, a darlin'. She can sing an' all. They was here early . . . rehearsin'.'

Ray walked into the club. It was only half full, with some obvious tourists and a few regulars. Ray threaded his way between the tables, stopping to have a quick word with people he knew. He crossed to the table where Alex Tupper sat with two other cozzers. The two brass with them were young, not bad looking.

'That piano player . . . he's a bit good,' said Tupper.

'The best.'

'You know Stan,' Tupper pointed to the other man. 'This is Eddie. Eddie Wesley . . . Ray Fox.'

Ray and Wesley shook hands. Tupper didn't bother to introduce the birds.

'Nice place,' Wesley said.

'It's a livin'.'

'Sorry to hear about Kenny,' Cullis said. He turned to the brass. 'Kenny Fox . . . the fighter,' he explained.

'Oh . . . honest, I read about him,' one of the girls said.

'Killed the other one.' The other girl knew the story too.

' 'Everso sad,' the first one commented.

'How's he taking it, Ray?' Cullis asked.

'Oh, triffic.' Ray didn't want to discuss it, especially with them. 'He's poppin' in fer a dance later.' He turned to Tupper. 'Can I buy you a drink, Alex?'

' 'Scuse me,' Tupper said to the others and followed Ray to the bar.

'Two Remies, Snoopy.'

'Sorry about that,' Tupper said as Snoopy turned away to get the drinks.

'They brass?' Ray asked, as if he didn't know.

'They owe me a favour,' Tupper smiled. 'I owe Eddie Wesley a favour . . . he fancied a two up.'

'Who is he?'

'DCI down from Manchester.' Tupper winked. 'He's cushtey.'

Snoopy arrived with the drinks. Ray took a slip of paper from his pocket with the registration number of the Westminster scribbled on it. He held it out to Tupper.

'Can you find out whose this is?'

Tupper took it, looked at it. 'Any special reason?' he asked.

Ray told him about the bricked windows and the car chase,

while Alan Haywood began his set playing 'Misty' and the club started to fill up.

It had been a hard day but Billy Fox was feeling a bit more relaxed. Joey had gone off to get his mates in the cabs looking out for Kenny and Vin was in his car scouring the manor for any sign of the boy. There wasn't much more to be done for the time being. Billy sat with Nan, going through his cases of highly prized jazz records. Connie sat in a chair, knitting.

'Nineteen sixteen was the first performance of New Orleans jazz in this country,' Billy explained. 'The Original Dixieland Jazz Band at the Hammersmith Palais.'

'I bet you was there, eh?' Nan loved Billy's enthusiasm, and enjoyed pulling his leg.

'You saucy . . .!' Billy laughed. 'I wish I 'ad been and that's a fact. That was history in the makin', jazz history at least. One thing I've promised meself before I pop off is to go and see New Orleans, Chicago.' He shook his head sadly. 'Probably too late, probably nothin' left of the great days . . . It's a long time ago now, a lifetime . . .'

Nan looked closely at a record she pulled from the case. She started to read the label, giggling. 'Miff Mole and his Molers Playing Shi Shim Shemmesha . . .' She stumbled over the words.

'Shim-Me-Sha-Wabble,' Billy said, straight out. 'Miff on trombone, Red Nichols on trumpet, Gene Krupa on drums.'

'Miff Mole and his Molers,' Nan interrupted, laughing. 'Sounds like a dentist.'

'There's another one in there: Sharkey Bonana and his Sharks of Rhythm,' Billy said.

'You're making it up!'

Connie looked up from her knitting. 'Not even Billy could make *that* up.'

'They're collector's pieces,' Billy said proudly.

'An' he can tell you who's playing on every one of them,' Connie told Nan.

'He ought to go on Mastermind.'

'They can't afford me,' Billy said.

They all laughed.

At the entrance to the club, Steve was paying off a cabbie who'd just delivered four punters. His commission was four quid a head and Steve peeled the notes off a thick roll.

'Keep 'em comin', Chuffa.'

'What's favourite? Still krauts and ragheads?'

'Anythink, as long as it's got a mouth an' a wallet.'

Chuffa laughed and took off. Steve suddenly saw Sheila watching him, but he couldn't believe it was her. At thirty-five, she was a very tasty London lady, three years' divorced from Ray. They'd always got on well, and he'd fancied her from a distance.

'Hello, Steve,' she smiled at him.

'I thought it was you. Then I thought, it can't be. I haven't seen you in what . . . three years?'

'Have I changed much?'

'Give us a twirl.'

Sheila twirled. Steve cast an expert eye over her.

'Lost a bit of weight,' he said.

'It's all that hard living I'm doing in Leicester,' Sheila said sarcastically.

'Leicester, Christ, that moochy 'ole. If they dropped an H-bomb on it, they'd do about five quids' worth of damage. What you doin' up there, gel?'

'Dying, slowly,' she said seriously. She paused. 'Is he in?'

'He never mentioned you was comin'.'

'He doesn't know.'

'Oh, yeah.' Steve sensed problems. 'Well, he's had a couple of dodgy old days, darlin'.'

'Poor Kenny,' Sheila said. 'I read about it.'

The internal phone buzzed in Ray's office. 'Yeah? What's up?'

'Nothin', least I don't think so,' Steve said. 'Sheila's on her way up.'

Ray was silent.

'I couldn't very well stop her,' Steve said after a moment.

'Yeah, yeah . . .'

'She's lookin' very lovely.'

'Go back to sleep.' As Ray dropped the receiver there was a knock at the door.

'It's open,' he said.

Sheila came in. They stood facing each other without speaking. There was still a strong attraction. They were both well aware of it. Sheila broke the silence.

'I was down to see Mum. I read about Kenny.'

Ray moved to the small bar, where he poured her a large vodka and lemonade.

'How is he, Ray?'

Ray shook his head. 'Not good,' he said.

Nan had gone home. Billy, Connie and Phil sat in the living room, still hoping to hear something from Kenny. They all looked tired but Billy was white with exhaustion.

'There's nothing we can do now,' Phil said at last. 'Why don't you two go to bed? I'll sit up in case Kenny shows.'

'Are you sure, love?' Connie said gratefully.

'I've got a lot of reading to do.'

Billy got to his feet reluctantly. 'If he ain't home by the morning we go to the police,' he said.

Ray and Sheila were having dinner in a discreet corner of the club. Alan Haywood was playing and Madeline singing an old Lady Holliday number, 'You've Changed'. Madeline was wearing a slinky white satin dress that displayed her body to some effect. Ray told Sheila about the problems with Kenny.

'You've been to the police?'

'Not yet.'

'Why not?' She was amazed.

'You know how many people are reported missin' every day . . . and how many turn up the next day, or the day after?'

'But these aren't normal circumstances. Kenny is under terrific strain, psychological strain!'

Ray played it down. 'He's probably back at Nan's or home by now.'

'They'd have phoned you.'

'It's only just gone midnight.'

'They could trace his car,' Sheila persisted. 'He's in his car and they could trace it.'

'Look, I promise you, if Kenny's not back by mornin', it's straight round the nick . . . no sweat.'

Sheila lit a cigarette. Ray watched Madeline, who sang directly to him. Sheila saw the look that passed between them and brought his attention back to her.

'I'm sorry,' she said.
'What for?'
'I suppose I always was a pushy cow?'
'Well . . .'
She acted offended. 'You weren't supposed to agree.'
'You said it.'
'I had to be – married to you.'
'What's that supposed to mean?'
'If you didn't stand up for yourself, know what you wanted, you got your life lived for you.'
'What are you on about?'
'The family. The Fox clan. King Billy.'
'Billy loved you, and Jenny. He'd've done anything for you.'
'Anything but really try to understand me,' she said wearily.
'He done his best,' Ray said angrily. 'He tried, we all tried. I know I tried like hell. It isn't easy with someone like you, Sheila . . . someone who doesn't really understand herself, doesn't *know* what she wants. Don't you rubbish Billy and the family for something that just wasn't their fault.'
Ray considered. 'Billy never forgave us for that divorce,' he said in a tight voice.
Sheila was about to reply when she saw Joey. The mood between them changed at once. They concealed the differences that were developing into a heavy scene. Joey was unaffectedly delighted to see Sheila and opened his arms to give her a big hug.
'Steve told me. I couldn't believe it. Come here, you.'
Sheila stood up.
'Hello sexy,' she said and hugged him. Joey's hug was a lovely-to-see-you hug. Sheila's was more desperate, as though she'd been starved of the affection she'd been used to as part of Ray's family.
Joey gave her bum a good old feel. 'You've lost a bit of weight . . . got a bony bum.'
'How are you, Joey?'
Ray pulled up a chair for Joey. Sheila sat down, Joey slumped into the chair.
'Knackered!' he replied. 'I just popped in to see Ray. He's told you about Kenny?'
'Is there any news?'
'Nothin'.'
'You hungry?' Ray asked.
'No, but I could give a terrible turking to a large scotch.'

Ray called Snoopy over. 'Snoops. Cointreau, Remy and a large Regal.'

'How are you then, darlin'?' Joey leaned back in his chair.

'Oh, all right. Missing London.'

'You do, don't yer? I mean, it's okay bein' away a couple of weeks, on holiday like. But any longer and you start gettin' withdrawal symptoms. It's Leicester, innit, where you are?'

'Just outside.'

'Well, you know what they say about Leicester?' Joey laughed. ' "The only good thing to come out of it is the road to London".'

Snoopy arrived with their drinks. Joey raised his glass to Sheila. 'Welcome home,' he said.

Sheila glanced nervously at Ray, who winked at her and turned for another look at Madeline. She was singing another Billie Holliday classic, 'I'm a Fool to Want You'. She really was very tasty, he thought.

Kenny was out in the countryside. He'd stopped at a few pubs on the way. He was driving along the country lanes like a maniac, radio blaring. On a tight bend he lost control of the car. It went into a spin and he fought to hold it. It ploughed into a shallow irrigation ditch and threatened to roll over. Its momentum carried it out and it came to a halt slewed across the lane. Kenny opened the door and ran out into the darkness to be violently sick.

Joey was telling Ray and Sheila a cabbie's story. They hadn't noticed the time passing. 'So there's poor old Barney's new hack, only got a thousand miles on the clock, impaled on the overriders of this bloody great American wagon, the front of it was a write-off . . . so there's Barney, all twenty stone of 'im, so cross he can't speak, and out trips this little baby-doll-blonde American sort. Y'know, all teeth, tits and credit cards. By this time there's steam comin' out of Barney's arse.' Joey paused to take breath.

'She looks at the wreckage, turns to Barney an' says, Gee . . . gee, I am so sorry . . .' Joey did a good imitation of an American female voice. 'Every time I put this car into first, it goes backwards!'

They all laughed. Alan Haywood and Madeline were finishing

their set with 'Don't Get Around Much Any More'. Joey checked his watch. 'I better get goin' . . . it's two,' he said.

'What time was *your* train?' Ray asked Sheila.

'I shall have to stay over. Didn't realise the time. Go back in the morning.'

'Use the flat.' Ray held out the key to her. 'Joey can drop you off on his way.'

Sheila considered for a moment. Joey didn't miss the look that passed between them. Sheila smiled and took the key.

'What about you?' She held up the key.

'Got a spare key in the office. 'Don't forget the dog. He'll remember you but take it easy goin' in. Let 'im have a good sniff.'

They all left the table and walked through the club. Alan Haywood and Madeline finished their last song and waited for Ray to come back. Madeline looked nervous, Alan lit a cigarette. He looked up when Ray walked over to the piano and nodded towards the door.

'I've not seen her before?' he said.

'She "Don't Get Around Much Any More".' Ray smiled.

'Someone special?'

'She was . . . once. More than special.'

Ray snapped out of his nostalgia. He turned to Madeline.

'He's right.' Ray nodded at Alan. 'You are ace.'

'Thank you.' She was delighted.

'I told you he had a great pair of ears.' Alan smiled at her.

'Hold on,' Ray said. 'Okay, she's great, but can I afford her?'

'I come real cheap,' Madeline said, afraid to lose the job.

'Not in my club, you don't. You get paid what you're worth.'

'It's the experience I want,' she said.

'Okay . . . we'll work something out.'

Madeline threw her arms round Ray's neck and gave him a kiss.

'You're a lover,' she said.

Phil sat up in Billy's house, reading and making notes. When his biro ran out, he searched round for something to write with. In one of the drawers in the living room he found a pencil. He was just about to close the drawer when he saw several kids' note-books held together with a thick elastic band. Curious, he took them out, slipped the band off and started to read the old-fashioned handwriting. He soon realised it was the beginning of Billy's account of his life, a kind of autobiography. It read:

> I've never been sure of the exact date I was born. There was a muck up with the birth certificate. It says I was born on the 7th May 1909, but my mother always insisted I was born a week before, on the first.

Phil took the books over to the chair and settled down to read them. He flicked forward a few pages:

> My father's name was Edgar but everyone called him Charlie. He was a rat catcher, the best there was so it was said. On a Saturday night he used to earn his ale by doing his act round the drinkers. He was something of a celebrity, folk used to come from all over to see Charlie perform, posh folk sometimes, real toffs. Rats was Charlie's life, rats was his passion, mark you that didn't stop him biting their heads off. That was Charlie's little turn, biting the heads of live rats.

Phil read on, absorbed, for a long time.

Ray let himself quietly into the flat. It was very late. He switched on the light, tiptoed to the bedroom. He opened the door and looked in. Sheila was asleep in his bed, her clothes carefully folded on a chair. Champ, the Alsatian, was curled up asleep at the bottom of the bed. Ray quietly closed the door and went back into the living room. He took off his jacket and tie, unbuttoned his shirt and kicked off his shoes. He crossed to the sofa and threw all the cushions on one end in preparation for kipping on it. Suddenly he realised Champ was in the room with him. He looked at the bedroom door, thinking he'd closed it. As he walked over, Sheila's voice came from the dark.

'Ray?'

'I thought you was asleep?'

'I was.'

Ray went in to the bedroom.

FOURTEEN

KENNY'S car was parked in the yard of a rundown farm, rusting equipment all around it.

There was still a hint of mist about, promising a warm day, when the early morning silence was broken by the clatter of a diesel engine. A farm labourer drove his tractor into the yard. On the back of the tractor stood a big man dressed in country clothes. He had a shotgun over his shoulder and a brace of rabbits, back legs tied together, in one hand. The man jumped down when he saw the parked car and crossed the yard to look inside. It looked empty from a distance, but Kenny was curled up uncomfortably on the back seat, asleep. He looked pale and drawn, flecks of vomit on his chin. The man banged on the top of the car with the butt of the shotgun, shouting at Kenny.

'Oi! You!' He went on banging maliciously. 'You in there!'

Kenny woke with a start, unsure where he was. When he sat up he banged his head on the roof. The man pulled open one of the car doors and leaned in.

'You're trespassing.' He had a Sussex accent, and the tone of his voice made it clear he was looking for trouble. 'Private, this is.'

Kenny began to recall what had happened. He got out of the car slowly, filling his lungs with the sweet morning air.

'You've got some explaining to do,' the man insisted belligerently.

'I got lost.'

'Lost was it?' He looked at the three-quarters finished bottle of scotch in the back of the car.

'Where am I?' Kenny asked.

'You in trouble?' The man saw the plastered eye and bruised face.

'What?'

'Been scrapping?' He pointed to Kenny's face.

Kenny's eyes went to the dead rabbits. One of them had lost half of its head; it was a bloody mess.

'I asked you a question,' the man said aggressively. 'You deaf or pig ignorant?'

Kenny went to get back in his car but the man held the gun

across the door to prevent him.

'You a London boy – one of them London hard boys?' The man was set on trouble, but Kenny didn't want to know. 'Is that what you are? Drunk, been fighting, in trouble?'

'Who is he?' the farm labourer called out.

'Looks like dirt to me,' the man called back. 'London dirt.'

Kenny's fists clenched. The man saw them and smiled.

'You want to scrap?'

Kenny just glared at him.

'Fancy it, do you?' The man was really pushing. 'Fancy your chances with me, boy?'

Kenny swallowed his anger, pushed past the gun and got in the car.

'London boys.' The man mocked him, taking him for a coward. 'Nancy boys, girl's handbags, that's all they are.'

Kenny started the car, slammed it into gear and accelerated out of the yard. The man dropped the rabbits, swung the shotgun expertly to his shoulder and aimed at the boot. He pulled both triggers. The man shouted like a kid playing cowboys as the hammers clicked on empty chambers.

'Bang! Bang!' he roared with laughter as Kenny's car disappeared round a bend in the lane.

Sheila came into the bedroom with a tray of tea. She was wearing Ray's dressing-gown with the cuffs turned back. Ray was already awake, on the phone to Billy.

'Ask for John Daysh,' Ray was saying. 'Y – S – H, he's a DI there, a mate of mine. Big, blond-haired guy . . . knows Kenny, big fan of Kenny's. How's Connie? Oh, good, yeah, see you. See you later, Pop.' He put down the phone.

'Any news?'

'Billy and Phil are just going round to report Kenny missing.'

'Is there anything I can do, Ray? I don't mind staying on a bit if there is.' She poured the tea.

'You don't sound in a hurry to get back?'

Sheila didn't reply. She passed Ray his cup of tea.

'Ain't it working out?'

She shrugged negatively.

'What's gone wrong?' Ray pushed.

'Everything. Oh, I suppose like most rotten marriages it's six of one, half a dozen of the other. You were right last night, I don't know *who* I am, *what* I am, what I *want*.' She paused. 'It would be very easy to blame him. I spent three years blaming you.'

Sheila lit a cigarette. 'When I met Derek I thought, he's everything Ray isn't. Quiet, cultured, sensitive, home every night. It was good, first few months. He was so . . . so caring.' She played with the end of her cigarette in the ashtray. 'I don't know what happened. That's a lie, I do but – how do you put it into words? How do you make sense of it? I sit for hours, just sit, staring out of the window feeling . . . *nothing*. Derek finds excuses for not coming home. I don't blame him. When we're together it's like two people living alone.' She smiled, self deprecatingly. 'I even do our laundry separately. I can't bear him to touch me.'

Ray listened sympathetically. He knew it wasn't easy for Sheila to tell him all this.

'What about Jenny?' he asked.

'She hates him.'

He was surprised. 'Jenny couldn't hate anyone.'

'She's changed, Ray. She's changed a lot. It's starting to really worry me.'

'The few times I've seen her she seems all right. At least she never said nothin'.'

'She's very loyal to me,' Sheila said, and smiled. 'She'd never let anyone know I'd made *another* mess-up. She never stops talking about you; it really upsets Derek. Sometimes I think she does it on purpose just to see how far she can push him. Has she ever asked if she can stay?'

'Stay?'

'Come and live with you?'

Ray was embarrassed. 'She knows that's not possible.'

'She's never hinted at it?'

'No . . . never.'

'I'm surprised.'

'Is that what she wants?'

'Part of it.'

'What's the rest of it?'

Sheila avoided the question and got up from the bed. 'Is it all right if I have a bath?'

'Sit down,' Ray ordered.

'I don't want to talk about it any more.'

'Sit down!' Ray reached out, grabbed her wrist and pulled her back down. 'We're talking about our daughter. She'll be sixteen soon and from the sound of it, if we ain't careful, she's goin' to end up a very screwed up sixteen-year-old.'

Sheila stayed very calm. 'Jenny's like me in many ways. When she can't face the truth she does what I do, believes what she wants to believe.'

'That you an' me are goin' to get back together again?'

'Why did you ask me if you already knew?'

'I wanted to hear *you* say it.'

'Why?'

'I wanted to watch your face.'

'Why?'

'It's the only way I've ever been able to tell if you're tellin' the truth.'

'I wouldn't lie about Jenny.'

'If you ever did . . .' There was an edge of menace in Ray's voice.

Billy and Phil were in a small, cluttered office at the local nick with Detective Inspector John Daysh. He was a tall, ambitious copper, with an air of efficiency.

'What was he wearing?' Daysh took notes in longhand.

'A leather jacket,' Billy said. 'New, only bought it last week. A spot it cost, *one hundred pounds* for a jacket.'

'What colour?'

'Light brown.'

'Tan,' Phil said, more exactly.

'Dark brown strides,' Billy went on. 'Boots, zip-up boots . . . at the side.'

'Pale blue shirt, no tie,' Phil added.

Daysh noted it all down. 'What about jewellery, rings?' he asked.

'His watch, good watch,' Billy said. 'That cost him I don't know how much.'

'And a gold chain,' Phil gestured round his neck, 'with a gold boxing glove on it.'

'Nan gave him that for his twenty-first.'

'Anything else?'

'He's got a couple of stitches in his eye. Left eye, plaster on it.' Billy said.

The mention of the cut made Daysh think back to the fight.

'It was a right sod. I couldn't get a ticket.'

'For the fight?' Billy looked at him.

'Even tried a couple of touts I know: sell out.'

'We've got to get him home, back trainin',' Billy said eagerly. 'He could have the title by Christmas.'

'Let's just find him first, Pop,' Phil interrupted. 'He may not want to fight again.'

This was sacrilege to Billy. He turned on Phil, angrily. 'Don't you start puttin' ideas in his head like that.'

'All I said was—' Phil started, but Billy interrupted him.

'He listens to you. Kenny listens to you, always has, ever since you was kids. Thinks you're something special. I know you, you've got some weird ideas, bloody funny ideas.'

'We didn't come here for a row,' Phil pleaded. 'We can have that at home.'

But Billy was in full flow. 'Education. It ain't all books, son. It ain't all books and lectures and Russian professors.'

'We're back to that, are we? I wondered how long it would take!'

Billy snorted. 'You just leave Kenny be. You leave him alone. Fillin' his head with bloody nonsense.'

Daysh looked embarrassed by this family flare-up, and he tried to bring the conversation back to the matter in hand.

'Did you bring a photograph?' he asked.

Billy and Phil avoided looking at each other. As Billy fumbled in his pocket for the picture of Kenny, Phil wondered why they were always coming into head-on collisions.

Kenny arrived at the coast. He headed for the beach and walked for a long time along the ribbon of sand, his jacket collar pulled up against the wind.

Then he walked back into the town. He looked through one of those shops selling everything from beach balls to dirty post-cards and found a pair of cheap sunglasses, big enough to cover his stitched eyebrow. He pulled off the plaster. With the glasses on, the stitched brow was completely hidden. Kenny went to the counter to pay for them. He rolled the piece of plaster into a sticky ball and dropped it on the shop floor.

Colin Street sat at the bar of Albert's pub, a large Gordon's and tonic in front of him, waiting for a chance to slip a few sly questions to Albert. His editor was pleased with the stuff on Kenny Fox and Street planned a big feature on boxing, highlighting Kenny's story. He lit a small cigar, finished his drink. Albert was testing a new barrel of bitter he'd just put on. He poured a couple of inches into a beer mug, held it up to the light to see it wasn't cloudy. Street pushed his empty glass forward on the bar.

'Yes, please,' he said.

Albert poured the test beer away and came to serve him.

'Same again, please.'

Street pointed to the photographs on the wall behind the bar. 'Isn't that Kenny Fox?'

Albert turned back with the large gin. 'Ice, no lemon, right?'

Street nodded. He tried again. 'Terrible, terrible what happened.'

Albert dropped two lumps of ice in the glass and put it in front of the journalist.

'Quite a gallery?' Street said as he held out a pound note for the drink, pointing to the photographs again. 'You a fan of his?'

'I'm a friend,' Albert said. 'An old friend.' He rang the price up on the till, scooped up Street's change and handed it to him.

Skegg, the Maceys' eyes and ears, moved up to the bar, pretending to study the racing fixtures in his paper. He was nursing a half of bitter and earwigging Street's conversation.

'I wonder how he must be feeling,' Street went on, playing the naive berk. 'Killing a man like that . . .'

'He's well choked,' Albert said at last. 'It's a hell of a knock back for him. It was a final eliminator, he was dead set for the title.'

'I suppose he'll chuck it in now?' Street hazarded.

'Not if Billy 'as any say in it he won't.' Albert was quite definite.

'His manager?'

'No, Billy's his old pot, his Dad.'

'Was he a boxer?'

'Billy?' Albert laughed. 'He could'a bin, clumped a few in his time. No, forty-five years in the Garden, Billy was. He's that bit older than me, but I remember when I was a kid and he was Kenny's age no one messed with Billy Fox.'

'He sounds quite a character?' Street prompted.

'King Billy they call him round 'ere. He's seventy now and he could still hook you over, no worry.'

Street ran a finger over his still slightly swollen nose where Billy had whacked him. Albert didn't know how close he was, but now at least he'd got him talking.

'I remember the first fight young Kenny had,' Albert went on. 'Schoolboy, he was, just fourteen. Amateur, of course. A minute and three seconds it lasted. He was a natural, hammer in both hands. I thought he was goin' to punch daylight through the other poor little sod.' Albert laughed as he remembered. 'The ref had to hold Kenny off. I thought Kenny was goin' to slip him one too!'

Skegg wasn't missing a word of their conversation, and it was an hour before Street left the pub and walked towards his car, parked in a side street. As he passed the doorway of a shop closed for rebuilding, George Macey stepped out in front of him.

'Oblige me, John?' He had an unlit cigarette in his mouth. Street, surprised, searched for his lighter. 'Got it somewhere,' he mumbled. Finding it, he lit George's cigarette.

'Could we have a word?' George asked.

'Hey! What the hell?' Street was bundled into the shop door before he knew what was happening. Frank Macey was waiting there. Across the road, Skegg was watching, keeping an eye out.

'Who are you?' George asked, sharply.

'Who are *you*?' Street threw back.

'He wants it the hard way,' Frank said to his brother.

Frank went to put his hand into Street's inside pocket for his wallet, but Street blocked him.

'You better give him a hand with his luggage,' Frank said to George. George dropped his hand and grabbed Street by the balls, squeezing hard.

'We only want a peep,' George remonstrated. Street gasped in agony. Frank hooked out Street's wallet, opened it and found the NUJ card.

'Colin Street. He's a journalist.'

'Well, well, well.' George was surprised. He released Street, who doubled forward, holding his balls.

'Who did you think I was?'

'We 'eard you was bein' a bit busy, askin' a lot of questions. A journalist, eh? You was givin' poor old Albert the gee, was you?'

'You knew who I was,' Street said suspiciously. 'All this is just an excuse to get nasty. Did Billy Fox send you?'

'King Billy!' Frank laughed at the thought.

'Did he?' Street asked angrily.

'Did he?' George asked Frank.

'That ole pig!' Frank laughed.

Street didn't understand. 'Then what, I mean, why?'

'Why should Billy send us?' George asked. ' 'Cos you're askin' a lot of questions about Kenny?'

'Don't he like that then?' Frank put in.

'Not a lot,' Street said.

'Why's that then?' George looked at Frank.

'He's protecting Kenny from the press. Won't let anyone near him, so I've got to get my story any way I can.'

'Interestin',' George grinned.

'Interestin',' parroted Frank.

'You're a very fortunate young feller,' George said. 'I mean, bumpin' into us. We can put you on to a very tasty little item, exclusive, about Kenny boy that no one knows yet. Leastways, none of your little mob – and that's no error.'

Street could smell a scoop.

'It'll cost,' George said.

'How much?'

'A ton.' George pointed to Frank and himself. 'Fifty-fifty.'

'That sounds reasonable, if it's good.'

'Oh, it's good. It's very, very good.'

'Good,' Street said.

'Good,' Frank echoed Street.

'He's an 'orrible piss-taker,' George told Street, who couldn't care less now he could smell a story.

'Killer Kenny's missin',' George began.

'Missing?'

'Lars night since,' Frank added.

'Some hounds from Charlie Locke's manor come over an' bricked Billy's windows,' George went on.

'Nearly bricked his ole gel as well,' Frank said smugly.

'While the family was out after 'em Kenny went tatas,' George continued.

'They're still lookin' for him,' Frank said.

'What time was this?'

' 'Bout seven,' George told him. 'He pops over to see Charlie's widow, but she was legless, give 'im a right slaggin'.'

'He steams off in his motor, not too happy, and it's Goodnight Irene,' Frank added. 'Hasn't been seen since!'

'You're certain about this?'

'Billy was at the nick this mornin' to report it, official,' George said.

'Which one?'

'Lavender Hill,' George smiled. 'If you want to check.'

'How do you know all this?'

'We're psychic,' George winked at his brother.

'Who are you?'

'He's Paul Newman and I'm Steve McQueen,' Frank said.

Street could see there was no point in pursuing it. The Maceys were going to tell him only what they wanted.

'Is there anything else?'

'Ain't that enough?'

'I'll have to check it. If you won't tell me who you are, how do I get the money to you?'

'You ain't got it on you?' Frank asked, amazed.

'A hundred pounds?'

'How much *have* you got?'

Street took out his wallet and counted. 'Fourteen pounds.'

Frank laughed, turned away. George gave him a look, took the fourteen quid and pointed out Skegg across the street.

'See that little reptile over there?'

Street remembered seeing him earlier. 'He was in the pub.'

'He'll be in the pub again, tonight at seven. You put eighty-six pounds, in an envelope, in his hand.'

'I may not be able—'

'Look, we done you a favour,' George said. 'You owe us eighty-six pounds.'

'All right. If you hear any other—' he started.

'We know where to come, don't we?' George interrupted.

As Street began to move away, George put a hand out to stop him. 'A nice *white* envelope.'

Street walked away. George counted out seven pounds, handed it to Frank. 'That wouldn't buy me an' 'aircut,' Frank complained.

'He's a mug. Let him think we're doin' it for the money.' George took a thick roll of notes from his pocket and added the paltry seven. They stepped out of the doorway, laughing, and crossed the road to give Skegg his instructions.

Kenny wandered aimlessly among the holiday crowds. The funny hat and candyfloss brigade were out in force in the bright sunshine. A group of women on a day trip, all half cut, sung and danced towards him. One of them lifted her skirt and flashed her knickers, the rest roaring their approval. She danced up to Kenny, grabbed him and started to waltz. Kenny was so far away, at first he didn't realise what was happening. The woman danced him round and round, her friends laughing and shouting her on. Kenny pulled away from her and pushed past them all. Wanting to get away from the crowds, he made his way to the back of the funfair. He stopped near a big diesel generator. A wire-mesh guard had been removed and the cooling fan scythed round. Kenny looked down at his offending hand, the one that killed Charlie Locke. He clenched it tight. Very slowly he advanced the fist towards the lethal blades. His face was impassive as he pushed the fist closer.

FIFTEEN

RAY took the call from Alex Tupper in his private office.

'You're in luck,' Tupper said. 'That Westminster checked out.'

'Got a name for me?'

'Seely, David Seely. He's a spiteful little bastard.'

'Any form?'

'Borstal twice, then a two for malicious wounding,' Alex said grimly. 'He was put up for that Essex supermarket blag but it got chucked. He's overdue. His two hangbacks are charmin' as well.'

Alex passed on some more details before he hung up.

A little later, Ray's white Jag passed the billiard hall and pulled up alongside the parked Westminster. He gave it the once over, then, satisfied it was the car, Ray drove the Jag down a side street. He turned round, so that the billiard hall and the Westminster could be seen from the Jag, and parked. When he got out he was carrying a holdall. He checked the deserted street, walked quickly to the Westminster. He tried the boot, it was locked. Checking again that he wasn't being watched, he put down the holdall, slipped a set of ringer keys from his pocket and soon had the boot unlocked. He unzipped the holdall, took out a sawn off shotgun. He hid it in the back of the boot, covering it with some sacking already there. He locked the boot and moved quickly away, carrying the empty holdall.

At the far end of the billiard hall, David Seely was playing snooker with one of the other faces who had bricked Billy's windows. He was twenty-two, good-looking and fancied himself. Another of the brick boys was keeping score. Ray went straight to a payphone in the near corner and dialled. He got the number right away.

'Alex?' he said quietly.

'Find him?'

'It's yer birthday. Got a present for yer.' Ray looked down the dingy hall with satisfaction. Seely and his two dopos were still playing. As he watched, Seely missed a black.

Ray left the hall and returned to his car, to sit and watch the Westminster. A car suddenly skidded to a halt beside it, followed closely by another. Alex Tupper and three big cozzers piled out of the two motors. They went straight to the back of the Westminster. One of the cozzers carried a crowbar and had the boot open in one hefty lever. Tupper leaned inside and soon came out with the planted shooter. He passed it to one of his team and they all moved towards the hall. Ray smiled and lit another cigarette.

The moment Tupper and his team walked in, Seely and his little mob knew it was the filth. Tupper went up to Seely.

'That Westminster outside, yours?'

'No, guv,' Seely lied. 'I ain't got a motor.'

'You're nicked,' Tupper told him.

'What in Christ's name for?'

Tupper reached back and took the shotgun from his man. He threw it on the table, scattering the balls. Seely's face registered honest amazement.

Tupper and his team dragged Seely and his mates out of the hall. They were still protesting when they were bundled into the waiting cars. Tupper paused for a moment. He lit a cigarette and looked up the road towards the parked white Jaguar. Its headlights flashed twice. Tupper chuckled and stepped into his car, which steamed off down the road after the other one.

Carol let herself into Ray's flat. She closed the door behind her. Ray's big Alsatian came up to greet her and she patted it.

'Hello Champ, hello boy.'

She heard the radio playing in the bathroom. She was in a very good mood, looking forward to seeing Ray. She crept noiselessly towards the bathroom like a kid playing a game, ready to make him jump. She pulled the door open and froze. Sheila was standing there still wearing Ray's robe. They looked at each other for a long moment.

'Where's Ray?' Carol asked.

'Out.'

'Who are you?'

'How did you get in?' Sheila was giving nothing away.

Carol held up her key to show her access to the apartment. 'Out where?' she asked.

'You sound like you have a right to know.' Sheila made it sound ironic. She switched off the trani and pushed past Carol into the main part of the flat.

Carol followed her. She saw the bedroom door open and looked in. She could see the unmade bed had been slept in by two. She slammed the door shut and turned on Sheila.

'Where did he pull *you* – at the club?' She paused. 'Does he know you're still here?' she asked venomously.

Sheila looked Carol up and down disdainfully. 'Was he expecting you?'

'Obviously not.'

'Oh dear, caught him out, have you?' Sheila smiled.

'Get dressed and get *out*.'

Sheila was unperturbed. 'I'll tell Ray you called,' she said sweetly.

Carol was thrown for a moment. It suddenly dawned on her who the woman in front of her might be.

'Are you her? Sheila?'

'What do we do now, shake hands?' Sheila asked coolly.

'What do you *want*?'

'You do sound suspicious. Or is it jealous?'

'Why don't you leave him alone?'

'He didn't want leaving alone.' Sheila glanced meaningfully towards the bedroom.

'There's nothing for you here.'

'What *is* your name?' Sheila asked irritably.

'Carol.'

'This wasn't my idea, Carol. I was down in London, read about Kenny. I went to see Ray. I've known Kenny since he was five. Ray gave me his key. He seems to have rather a lot of keys.'

'So you've *seen* him!' Carol wasn't placated. 'Why are you still hanging around?'

'Does he pull many birds from the club?' Sheila asked maliciously.

'I don't know. I don't ask. I don't care,' Carol said wildly.

Sheila smiled. 'You're a liar,' she said.

Skegg was sitting close to the door of Albert's pub when Street came in to pay off the Maceys' money. Street passed a white envelope to him and had a few words. Albert had been in the cellar and came up just in time to see Street going out and Skegg pocketing the envelope.

A few minutes later Billy, Vin and Joey came in. They'd been hanging around Billy's house all evening, hoping for news of Kenny. Connie had finally packed them off for what Billy called a 'quick half' but which usually took a lot longer. On their way in they'd spotted Street getting in his car. As they walked to the bar, Skegg slipped out unnoticed. Albert came up, pleased to see them.

'Evenin' Billy, didn't expect you tonight. How's Kenny?'

'I'll tell you in a minute. A young feller with whiskers just in?'

'In and out,' Albert said. 'Didn't even buy a drink. He was in here earlier.'

'Today?' Vin asked.

'This mornin'.'

'He's a reporter,' Joey put in.

'Oh no!' Albert sounded guilty. 'The snakey bastard never said nothin' about bein' a reporter.'

'You look sick, Albert,' Vin said.

'I'm sorry, Billy. He got me talkin' 'bout Kenny, you, the family. I thought 'e was just a punter, seemed a nice feller. You know what I'm like when I start rabbitin'.' Albert pointed to his mouth. 'Blackwall Tunnel, innit?'

'Ah, forget it,' Billy said. 'Ain't your fault. But if he comes in again—'

'I'll put him in plaster,' Albert clenched a massive fist. 'Hey, hold up a minute—'

Big Albert moved to one side so he could see past the Fox trio to the table where Skegg had been sitting. Skegg was gone, an unfinished pint left on the table.

'He was talkin' to the cockroach, over there.' Albert nodded to the empty seat.

'Looks like he left a bit swift,' said Vin.

'The reporter give him somethin', an envelope. He was in this mornin' too,' Albert suddenly remembered and pointed down the bar. 'Sittin' there.'

'Wiggin' everythin' you was tellin' that jackal,' Billy said knowingly.

'I could cut me tongue out, Billy.'

'You'll have to go and bite the altar rails on Sunday, my son.' Billy laughed. 'It's goin' to cost you three large scotches.'

As Albert went to get the drinks, Billy turned to Vin and Joey. 'I think we're going to have a little parlez-vous with that creature.'

When Ray got back to his flat, Carol was waiting for him. She stormed into the bedroom, where everything was exactly as Ray and Sheila had left it that morning. Ray followed her in.

'Who do you think you are?' Carol shouted. 'I'm a person – a person, Ray. I don't mind the little scrubbers, they don't bother me. But *her*!'

Carol started tearing at the bed. 'Her! That—'

Ray made no attempt to stop Carol tearing the bed to pieces. She was close to tears. 'That scheming slut!' Carol had exhausted herself wrecking the bed. She slumped down on the bare mattress.

'Have you finished?' Ray asked quietly.

Carol sobbed. She wouldn't look at Ray. He lit a cigarette, walked across and held it out to her. She slapped it out of his hand. It landed on one of the sheets lying on the floor. Neither of them made any move to retrieve it. They both watched as it started to burn a hole in the sheet. Suddenly Carol darted forward, picked up the cigarette and rubbed out the singe.

Ray spoke after watching Carol in silence. 'I'm only goin' to tell you this once, so you better listen, Carol. I do what I want, with who I want, *because* I want. I had thirteen years of this sort of shit from *her*. If you don't like the way I am, go and find yourself a munchkin like she did. I don't need this, darlin'. I've got enough to worry about with Kenny on the trot. So, you make that bed and get hold of your mouth!'

Ray turned and left the bedroom. Carol stood quite still looking at the mess of the bed, trying to decide what to do. She picked up the sheet as if to make up the bed. Slowly and deliberately she started to tear it.

Kenny was getting drunker and drunker. He was in a seaside pub where he'd spent half the night. He slumped at a corner table, paying no attention to the group of hounds playing a noisy game of darts. He still wore the shades, which looked ridiculous in the well-lit pub.

Kenny finished his drink, picked up the glass and lurched to the bar. 'Nurse,' he called.

The barman looked at him irritably and walked down the bar. 'Haven't you had enough, son?'

'You, you think I can't . . . can't pay for it?' Kenny was clearly the worse for wear.

'It isn't that, son.'

'I can pay for it, I can pay for it.' Kenny awkwardly pulled a small pile of notes from his pocket and dropped them on the bar.

'See . . . seeeeeeee . . .'

'Okay, so you can pay for it.' The barman wished he hadn't said anything. 'It's your liver.' He picked up Kenny's glass, turned to the optics and poured a single scotch.

'Large one!' Kenny said, watching closely.

The barman put in another tot.

'An' one for the Queen, eh? Go on, whack it in,' he said as the barman hesitated.

The man put in the third tot and laid the drink down on the bar. Kenny pushed all the money at him. 'An' one for yerself, you're a good ole boy,' Kenny mumbled. 'A good ole nurse . . . I like you. You're all right, you are.'

The barman took two pounds, rang it up, got Kenny's change. He picked up all the money, leaned over the bar and put it in Kenny's jacket pocket. 'That's the last one I'm going to serve you, son.'

Kenny grinned lopsidedly, picked up his monster drink and tottered back to his corner seat. A tacky bird in her early twenties, not unattractive in a rough sort of way, had been watching Kenny for some time from a nearby table. She kept her eye on him now as he took a large gulp of scotch, and half fell back on his chair.

Kenny staggered out of the pub and leaned against the wall to steady himself. He moved erratically down the road. Everything seemed to be out of focus, the backstreet was contorted into strange shapes and angles like looking into the crazy mirrors in a funfair. Kenny found himself falling through space to roll over on his back, laughing as he stared up at the black slate of the sky. For a brief moment he remembered the old greyhound bitch pushing her face into his vision. Out of focus, another face, a woman's face, was leaning over him.

'Come on, love.' The voice sounded miles away. 'Find you like this, they'll pinch you. Help you up.'

The girl got him to his feet.

'Who are you?'

'I was in the pub.'

'Nan?' Kenny was confused.

'My name's Rita.'

'You're not Nan?'

'Rita,' she said patiently.

'Rita? I don't know no Ritas.'

'Come on, before they pinch us both,' the girl said, putting one of Kenny's arms round her shoulder, and then half walked, half carried him down the street. They passed Kenny's car.

'Whoooooaaaaaaaa!' he shouted.

'What's the matter?'

'My motor, that's my motor motor.' Kenny giggled. 'Motor motor motor car.'

Kenny got out his keys, turned back and tried to unlock the door, fumbling.

'Give it here.' Rita took the keys, unlocked the driver's door. Kenny started to get in.

'You can't drive,' Rita said forbiddingly.

'Sleep, goin' to sleep,' he mumbled.

'Here?'

'Sleep.' Kenny was almost out.

'Aren't you staying anywhere, a hotel, bed and breakfast?'

Kenny shook his head slowly.

'Nowhere?' Rita asked.

'Sleep, sleep, got to get some kip.'

'D'you want ter come home with me? You can sleep there. I got a big bed, eh?'

Kenny nodded. He could hardly keep his eyes open. He crawled over the driver's seat to the passenger side. Rita got in behind the wheel. She pushed Kenny out of the way, slammed the door and started the car.

She drove into the overgrown drive of a big old house. It was boarded up, deserted, waiting for demolition. She stopped the car, cut the lights, and eventually coaxed Kenny out, half asleep. She practically had to carry him into the house. It was pitch dark inside. Rita kicked the door shut and blindly but knowingly walked Kenny into one of the downstairs rooms. She propped him against a wall and left him while she went over to the fireplace and lit a couple of candle stubs standing on the mantelshelf.

The room filled with muted light to show Kenny still leaning obediently against the wall. In one corner of the room there was an iron-framed bed, with a damp mattress on it. In another corner empty beer cans and mildew covered a pile of take-away food boxes. The squatters who had used this place had left long ago.

Rita came back to Kenny, who was too drunk and tired to do or say anything as she stripped off his expensive leather jacket.

'Have to take this off,' she murmured.

Kenny obeyed her like a child.

'Don't want to go messing it up, do you, creasing it all up?'

When Rita had the jacket off, she led him to the bed and let him flop down on it. As soon as he hit the mattress he was out cold, face down. Rita made sure he could breathe, then started to go over him for money. She took his boots and put them with the jacket, took off his watch, tried to undo the clasp of the gold chained boxing glove around his neck. Kenny rolled over, stopping her, so she pulled the chain hard until it broke off. When she had everything of value, Rita gathered it all together in a bundle and blew out the candles. She lit her lighter, took a last look at Kenny and walked out of the ratbag room, carrying the bundle of stolen gear.

SIXTEEN

IT was early morning, but Kenny's car was already being prepared for respraying in a backstreet garage. Easy, a thirty-year-old ringer with a pock-marked face and long greasy hair, worked on it deftly and urgently. Most of the chrome had been removed. Masking tape and newspaper covered the rest and the windows. There was a bang on the locked door.

'Easy, come on. It's me, Lee.'

Easy moved slowly to the door, threw back the heavy bolt and opened the door within a door. Lee came in, a small-time layabout who dealt in dope and pills round the clubs and discos. He was a strutter with an imitation of the old Rod Stewart cockerel, dyed blond haircut to match his style. He was wearing Kenny's leather jacket but he was taller than Kenny, so the sleeves weren't long enough and it didn't really fit.

Lee looked at the car. 'Ain't wastin' much time.'

'That's the name of the game, cocker. In and out, bang, no messin'.'

'What colour you goin' ter do it?'

'Diarrhoea yellow,' Easy grunted.

Lee pulled a face. ' 'Orrible.'

'The mugs love it.'

Lee made a suggestion. 'Deep purple with silver flashes.'

'And who do I knock it out to? Some lobe who thinks he's Hunt the Shunt? First night out, showin' off to his bird, wraps it round the pier. The cozzers sit at his bedside till he regains consciousness, the snide logbook in their hand. "Who did you get the car from, Chummy?" and it's me on cold cocoa for a couple of years. Be sensible.'

Lee hadn't expected this tirade. He shrugged. 'I don't give a toss what colour you do it. All I come for was me money.'

Easy walked to his jacket, hanging up on a nail. He took a bundle of ten pound notes from the inside pocket and threw it to Lee.

'Four hundred,' he said.

Lee started to count the money.

Easy was offended. 'Get out of here,' he snapped.

'Just checkin'.'

'You . . . lump!'

Lee stopped counting, put the money away with a smile. When he left, Easy bolted the door again. When the door was shut Lee turned and gave Easy the finger. He got into an old van and drove off.

He pulled up near a kid's playground. He hooted and Rita ran over to get in. She closed the door and turned to Lee excitedly.

'Get it?'

'No.' Lee shook his head. 'The bastard wasn't there.'

Rita's face clouded. 'What about the car?'

'That neither.'

'What are we going to do, Lee?'

'What can we do?' He shrugged. He took the cigarette from Rita's fingers and dragged on it.

She was angry. 'I was counting on that bread.'

'I can lend you a few quid.' Lee casually took the four hundred pounds from his pocket and held it out. 'How much do you need?'

'You rotten pig!' Rita realised he'd been geeing her up and went to grab the money. Lee snatched it back.

'Greedy,' he said. They fought like two kids over the bundle of notes and ended up laughing and giggling, Rita's shirt front ripped open. Lee pushed the money into the shirt to finish the game. He took her cigarette and settled back to smoke what was left while she divided the money. She passed him his two hundred.

'What are you going to do with it?'

'Invest it.'

'No, serious?'

'I've got a connection with some very reasonable pharmaceutical merchandise.' Lee took a small tube of 'samples' from his pocket, held them up for Rita to see. They were mostly barbs, nembutal and seconal, and speed, ritalin and preludin.

Rita needed some cigarettes, so Lee pulled the van up at a seaside newsagents. She was away a few minutes. When she came back, she was holding up a morning newspaper for him to see. There was a front page story by Colin Street, with a photograph of Kenny.

'That's *him*,' Rita said.

'Who?'

'*Him!* You're wearing his jacket.'

Lee unwrapped one of the cigarette packets Rita had brought

and checked the photograph. 'You sure?'

'How many of them pills have you taken?' Rita asked.

'Kenny Fox,' Lee read. 'He's a boxer.'

'His eye was cut, stitched. I thought he'd been in a punch up.'

Lee lit two cigarettes. 'You dumped him at the house?'

'Yeah.'

'Reckon he could still be there?' Lee handed Rita one of the fags.

'It's still early, could be, he was pissed witless. I had to carry him. Why?'

Lee smiled, dropped the van into gear and gunned it away.

Inside the derelict house it was dark even in daytime. Lee carried two cups of take-away coffee in polystyrene cups with lids. Rita peered round the door into the room where she'd left Kenny.

'He's still crashed out,' she whispered excitedly. 'It's so dark in there he won't be able to see me.'

'Magic,' Lee said. 'Hold these.'

He passed her the cups. He lifted the lid of one cup, dropped in three nembutals from his tube of pills. He put the top back, took the cup from Rita and swilled it round till he was sure the pills were dissolved. Then he passed it back to her. She went into the room, then came back at once. 'The jacket,' she said. 'He might notice.'

Lee slipped it off reluctantly and Rita took it in. She was gone a few minutes and Lee made himself comfortable on the stairs, amusing himself blowing smoke rings. He could hear fragments of conversation as Rita fed Kenny the coffee, pretending to be looking after him. Kenny sounded barely coherent. When she came out Rita was carrying the two coffee cups. She tipped one upside down to show Kenny had drunk all the doped coffee. Lee got up and walked to the far end of the hallway, so that he could talk to Rita without Kenny hearing.

'How long will it take?' she asked.

'Not long.'

'How much did you put in?'

'Enough.' Lee smiled knowingly.

Rita was alarmed by the smile. 'You don't know the meaning of the word.'

'He'll sleep like a baby.'

'As long as that's *all* he does,' Rita said.

They almost had to carry Kenny down the stairs to the cellar. He had his jacket draped round his shoulders and was just about conscious, but he was a dead weight. They had candle stubs, stuck with wax to empty beer cans, to light their way, but Lee stumbled and hot wax flicked on his hand.

'Bastard!' He grimaced and dropped the candle. It went out.

'Leave it. We can see with mine,' Rita said.

They manhandled Kenny, head lolling on his chest, down the last few stairs and along a short passageway to a door. Lee kicked it open. The cellar had thick stone walls, no windows. A load of old furniture had been abandoned and they dumped Kenny into a disintegrating armchair. He just slumped there, fast asleep. His jacket slipped to the floor. Rita picked it up and covered him with it.

'What you doin'?' Lee asked in amazement.

'It's freezin' down here.'

Lee snatched the jacket off Kenny. 'That's *mine*.'

'But he's shivering,' she protested.

'Tough.' Lee put on the jacket.

'We can't just leave him like that. It doesn't fit you anyway,' she said as an afterthought.

Lee took Rita's candle and had a good look round the cellar. He found an old curtain, mildewed and motheaten, and threw it at Rita. 'Tuck him up,' he said mockingly.

Rita felt the curtain. It was damp and it stank, but she thought it was better than nothing and began to wrap it around Kenny.

'You'd make a lovely mummy,' Lee sneered.

'Why don't you go and play with yourself?'

Lee crossed to have a look at the door. There was no lock or bolt. 'How are we goin' to lock this door?'

Rita thought. 'Tie it up from the outside?'

Lee went off to find some rope. Upstairs in the kitchen he'd seen an old wooden airing frame on a system of pulleys. He took out a switch knife and cut the rope holding the frame to the ceiling. It crashed down in a cloud of dust. When he got back to the cellar, Rita was still fussing with the curtain, arranging it round Kenny. He held up the rope.

'Let's get out of here.'

Rita was a bit slow to leave.

'I think you fancy him.'

'He's better looking than you,' Rita replied caustically.

Lee tied the door up on the outside. He made a pretty good job of it and tested it to see it was secure.

'Get out of that!' he said with satisfaction.

'I suppose this is kidnapping?' Rita was having second thoughts.

'I suppose it is.' The idea appealed to Lee, it sounded big-time.

'If we get caught—' Rita began.

Lee knotted his fingers in her hair, twisted her head sideways.

'Don't you go girlie on me now,' he said sadistically.

She shouted with pain.

'You just remember, ravishin' Rita. You tapped him up, brought him here, ripped his money, his gear and his motor. So don't pretend you've fallen off a Christmas tree!'

He let go her hair and she slapped his hand away. 'Sometimes I hate you, you horrible bastard!'

'Yeah . . . I know.' Lee smiled.

Billy came out of his front room to answer the phone.

'Hello?' There were pips, the sound of money pushed in.

'Is that Kenny Fox's house?'

'I'm his father.'

'Good, 'cos I've got news for you, dad.'

'You got a name?'

'Just shut your mouth and listen. I know where Kenny is, don't I?'

'Where?'

'That's goin' to cost you.'

'Why don't you go to see a doctor, son, you're sick.' Billy decided it was another crank call.

'You better listen, old man.'

'How many bastard calls like this do you think we've already had?' Billy was about to dump the receiver, but something about the voice kept him listening. Phil and Connie stood behind him.

'The number of his driving licence is A8751985,' the voice continued. 'His bank service card number is 601533 . . . and what about this then? A photograph of him with a chick, looks like they're on holiday. Foxy lady . . . get that? *Foxy* lady, that's a joke, dad. Oooooh, she looks a bit of a teaser.' The caller was enjoying himself.

'You've got Kenny's wallet,' Billy said quietly.

'I've got *Kenny*, mister, and like I said, you want him back, it's goin' to cost.'

'How much?' Connie and Phil knew something was up. They stood as close as they could, trying to hear the voice.

'How much?' Billy repeated.

'I'm not greedy, say five hundred.' The voice went on to give Billy some very specific instructions.

Ray hammered down the coast road in his Jag. Vin sat beside him, studying an AA map book on his lap. Billy was in the back. They were all very tense.

'I've got it,' Vin said. 'Just off the A21.'

'How much further?' Ray asked.

'About twenty miles.' Vin looked up at Ray. 'Maybe Phil was right, maybe we should've gone to the law?'

'We can handle it. We've always handled our own aggravation. We don't want *this* all over the front page,' Ray said tightly.

'That bag of worms, Skegg,' Billy said. 'He must of put that reporter on to Kenny goin' missin'.'

'We'll have to ask him, won't we?' Ray asked with menace.

They drove on in silence. Billy could see Ray was very worked up. 'When we get there, we do it his way,' Billy said. 'The way he said.'

'We'll see.'

'You just listen to me, Ray,' Billy insisted. 'Okay, he might be a chancer, he might have found Kenny's wallet—'

'He's a stiff, a cheap little slag!' Ray snapped. '*Five hundred*, he's got to be *nothin'* to ask five hundred!'

'We can't take chances.' Billy was worried about Ray. 'You listening, Ray?'

'All right, all right, we do it your way.'

'*His* way,' Billy corrected.

Ray put his foot down and the car surged forward.

Lee's van was parked off the road, hidden behind trees and bushes. Lee and Rita waited nervously, smoking. They overlooked the road near a lay-by, but couldn't be seen from it. Rita was the first to see the Jag approaching. It slowed down.

Lee whistled softly. 'Look at that car. Maybe I should have

made it a thousand.'

The Jag pulled in to the lay-by.

'It's them, it's got to be,' said Rita.

'Three of 'em,' Lee counted.

Ray, Billy and Vin just sat in the car. They looked about, as discreetly as they could.

'See anything?' Ray asked.

Vin checked. 'No.'

'Nothing,' Billy said.

Ray glanced over to the trees and bushes. 'If he's here, he's watching us. Could be over there.'

Billy was anxious not to take any chances. 'Let's get on with it,' he said. He took a brown envelope from his inside pocket and started to get out of the car. Ray stopped him.

'You stay here, Pop. I'll do it.'

'Why?'

'Just in case.'

Billy shook his head. 'If he's out there, he's expectin' to see me.'

Lee and Rita watched as Billy got out of the car, carrying the envelope. They whispered to each other, though there was no need.

'He's got it, he's got the envelope,' Rita breathed.

'Magic! Bloody magic.'

Billy looked about him once again.

'Taking his bloody time,' Lee said.

'You sure he can't see us?'

'I told the old prat.' Lee was angry. 'I warned him – no tricks.'

Billy headed for a litter basket, dropped the envelope inside. He turned and walked back to the car. Lee and Rita watched Billy's every move.

'Now piss off, old man,' Lee whispered.

Billy had a last look round, got into the car and it began to move away down the road. Rita and Lee could hardly believe it was all going so smoothly. The Jag disappeared when the surrounding trees blocked it from view.

'Give them five minutes.' Lee checked his watch. 'Then you go out and collect it.'

'They might double back?'

'We'll make sure they haven't.'

'Another *five hundred*,' Rita said greedily.

'I thought you didn't want to go through with it, kidnapping you said?' Lee said playfully.

Rita put her arms round his neck. 'I didn't know you were such a clever feller.' She kissed him, as much in relief as anything.

'What a team,' Lee said. 'We'll be drivin' a motor like that soon.'

In a little while, Rita stepped out of the van. She kept to the security of the trees until she could see the road was clear in both directions. She crossed the road quickly and collected the envelope from the litter basket. When she had it in her hand, Lee started the van and drove through the bushes out on to the road. The passenger door swung open and Rita jumped in. Lee powered the van away in the opposite direction to the Jag.

Rita tore open the envelope and took out the five hundred pounds ransom. She squealed with delight.

'We've done it. We've done it, Lee!'

She threw her arms around him, kissed him. The van almost went off the road but Lee corrected the swerve. He pushed her away roughly.

'*Count* it!' he shouted.

SEVENTEEN

RAY'S Jag was parked near a phone box on the edge of a village. Billy was in the box, waiting for the call. Vin held open the door, Ray paced round restlessly.

'Twenty minutes!' Ray checked his watch, flicked his half-smoked cigarette to the ground and stamped on it.

'Must be the right box,' Vin said. 'It's the only one.'

'It's the right box,' Billy said grimly.

Ray lit another cigarette. 'I think we've been cattled.'

Vin tried to calm him. 'There ain't much more we can do but wait.'

'Twenty minutes!' Ray flared. 'I said it was smelly. It's a get-up, he's done us over. He must be laughing himself sick!'

'He'd need to collect the money, then get to a phone,' Billy pointed out.

'I'm goin' back to see if he's picked up the money.'

'You're staying here,' Billy ordered.

But Ray got in his car. Billy came out of the phone box angrily. 'Ray!' he shouted.

The phone rang suddenly. Billy rushed back into the box and lifted the receiver.

'Yeah?' Vin and Ray crammed into the box. 'Hello? Are you there?'

'You don't sound very happy, dad?' Lee was enjoying Billy's nervousness.

'You got the money?'

'What money?'

Billy knew Lee was trying to wind him up. 'We've paid you.'

'Five hundred?'

'That's what you asked for.'

'If I'd known you was loaded—'

'Where's Kenny?'

'I mean, that blizzard-white four point two, now that's a real dude's tool, a solid grand set of wheels.'

'You won't squeeze no more, son, so forget it,' Billy said tightly.

'Have I asked for more?'

'Where's Kenny?'

'Er, er. Now let me see . . .'

Billy realised he was dealing with a nut. He was on tenter-hooks but he stayed calm. 'Don't mess me about, son.'

'You really are wired up aren't you, old man? Be nice, polite. Say please.'

'Please,' Billy said, swallowing.

'I don't hear you.'

'*Please!*'

'Sir.' Lee giggled.

Billy looked at Vin and Ray. They could guess what was happening.

'Sir,' Billy said.

'Now together.'

'Please, sir.'

'That's much better. Now I'm only goin' to say this once, so you better be ready.'

Billy waved to Vin and Ray for something to write with. Vin quickly produced a pen and a used envelope.

'I can hear your heart beating . . .' Lee was still drawing it out.

The Jag pulled off the road into the drive of the derelict house which looked even more decayed in daylight. They all piled out. Vin and Ray kicked in the front door, and Billy carried a torch to light their way down the cellar steps.

Vin shivered. 'Bloody freezin' down here.'

'This is it.' Billy's torchlight caught the rope tying the cellar door.

'Kenny?' Ray and Vin called out at the same time. There was no reply.

'You in there, Kenny?' Billy shouted. He started frantically to untie the knot in the rope.

'Let me, Pop.' Vin had a penknife and cut the rope away. They moved quickly into the cellar, Billy flashing the torch beam over the room. Kenny was sitting on the floor, slumped back against a wall.

'Careful, he might be hurt,' Ray warned.

'Lift him up,' Vin said.

Together they carefully lifted Kenny to his feet. He was just about conscious.

'He's frozen stiff,' said Vin.

Ray whipped off his jacket, wrapped it around Kenny's

shivering body. 'Give me the torch.'

Billy passed the torch and Ray shone it on the deathly pale face. Kenny blinked like a hibernating animal and tried to shield his eyes.

'He's well out of it, look at his eyes.'

'I wonder what the scum bag give him?'

Billy put his arms round Kenny. 'You're not hurt?'

Kenny shook his head.

'Let's get 'im out of this 'ole!' Ray said angrily.

Ray had the car engine running, the heater fan blasting hot air inside. Billy had Kenny in the back, wrapped in a travelling rug, and was trying to rub some life back into Kenny's body. Ray passed over a small bottle of brandy from the glove compartment.

'Try and get some of this down him.'

Billy unscrewed the top and held it to Kenny's mouth.

'Lucky he's a fit boy,' Vin said. 'Another few hours in that ice-box and he could've bin a gonner.'

'That filthy slag, leavin' him in that state!' Ray was so angry he shook.

Kenny was recovering slowly. The brandy helped.

'Let's get him home,' Billy said.

'Shouldn't we take him to hospital?'

Kenny heard Vin. 'No, no hospitals!' he said nervously. 'I've had enough of bloody hospitals!'

'All right, son, we're goin' home.' Billy was almost in tears. He cradled Kenny in his arms. 'Let's go, Ray.'

But Ray started to get out of the car. 'You drive, Vinnie.'

Vin knew Ray didn't let anyone drive his car.

'You take Pop and Kenny home. I've got business here.'

Billy and Vin knew exactly what he meant.

'Leave it, Ray,' Vin said. 'We've got Kenny, let's go home.'

'Swallow it?'

'That's right.'

'This is personal now,' Ray said. 'That nonse is bang in trouble. You get 'ome, I'll see you later, eh?'

'I'll come with you,' Vin offered.

'What for?'

'You may need some help.'

'I've got all the help I need down here.'

'Tell him Pop.' Vin appealed to Billy.

'He wouldn't listen.'

Vin shrugged. 'I tried.' He moved into the driving seat. Ray leaned forward for a parting word with Kenny.

'Take it easy, kid. You'll soon be home.'

'That bird's name, I think I've remembered it,' Kenny said. 'Rita . . . Rita.'

'Good boy.' Ray looked at Billy. 'They've fucked with the wrong family, Pop.'

Billy nodded. 'You know where we are if you need us.'

Ray slammed the door, Vin started the big saloon down the drive and out into the road. Billy turned and gave Ray a brief glance of approval before the car was gone.

Rita's flat was small and squalid, just a bedsit with a curtained-off kitchen area. There were clothes everywhere. A kitten was curled up asleep on a pillow of the unmade bed and the sheets hadn't seen a laundry in weeks. Some 'True Confessions' magazines lay on the bed, below a poster of Robert de Niro. Lee and Rita came in. Lee flopped on the bed, smoking a big cigar, and narrowly missed the kitten. He had three more cigars in silver tubes sticking out of his pocket.

'In words of one . . . *what a giggle*!' He took a handful of notes from his pocket and threw them up in the air. They fluttered down like giant confetti and settled on the bed. Rita was still a bit apprehensive.

'What's the matter with you?'

'I hope he was all right when they found him.'

'Stick or twist, it's done now.' He picked up a fist of notes from the bed. 'Smell it.'

'It was a laugh.' Rita forced a smile.

'We're goin' out tonight.' Lee grabbed her wrist and pulled her down on the bed.

'To celebrate?' She giggled.

'To get pissed.'

He rolled on top of her.

'We're goin' to *celebrate* now!' Holding the cigar in one hand he started to undo the belt of Rita's jeans with the other.

Ray walked into the brash, noisy, amusement arcade. It was full of holiday kids from the London ghettos, feeding their saved-up money into the greedy machines. The din was deafening, a mixture of Muzak, clanging bells, electronic rifle shots and one-armed bandits disgorging payouts. Ray went up to an old lady, cocooned in a tiny booth and handing out piles of change. He said something and she pointed to a door at the far end of the arcade marked 'Office'. Ray walked down there. He knocked and a voice came from inside.

'I'm busy!'

Ray opened the door.

'You need your ears syringing?' Dave South was bending over a stripped-down one-armed bandit, trying to repair it. The office was a cramped little room.

'I don't think so,' Ray answered. Dave turned. He was a Bermondsey lad, a bit younger than Ray. He wasn't big, but he was the sort you don't look at twice without good reason. One of eleven kids, he'd learned to take care of number one at a very early age.

'Well I'll be buggered,' he said when he saw Ray.

'Hello, Dave.'

'Ray Fox.'

'How are yer?' Ray offered his hand.

'Tickin' over.' Dave shook it. 'What about you, still runnin' that club in The Jungle?'

'Until I get a proper job.' Ray smiled.

'How did you know where to find me?'

'Steve told me.'

'Stevie Judd?'

'He's workin' for me now, mindin' my place . . . he's a diamond.'

'How long ago was it?' Dave asked. 'You an' me?'

'Sixty-nine.'

'It can't be.'

'It's goin' to take me a long time to forget that cesspit,' Ray said.

'Was a bit of a pigpen,' Dave agreed. 'Remember that screw you done up? Big, evil bastard. You wrecked 'im?'

'Didn't do me no good, did it though? Lost sixty days remission.'

'What you doin' down 'ere?'

'Rat catchin'.' Ray took fifty quid from his pocket, held it out to Dave. 'An' I need a bit of 'elp.'

Dave looked at the money, he could well do with it.
'You can put that away,' he said.

Ray and Dave walked along the pier, among the small groups of men fishing and idling. Dave introduced Ray to Lol, a small, tubby man in his late forties. They shook hands. Lol, sucking on a metal-stemmed pipe, sized Ray up. They walked along to the pier bar, sitting at a table well away from the other drinkers.

'Rita?' Lol repeated. He had dodgy eyes and a car salesman's smile. 'What sort of age?'

'Early twenties.'

'Only Rita I know works in a chippie and she's so old she's got stretch marks on her lips. What time was this number nicked?'

'Late last night.'

'They'll have it stripped down and going out in boxes, or sprayed up with snide plates on it by now.'

'Who, Lol?' Dave asked. 'Any idea who?'

'It ain't exactly this year's model, is it? I mean, it's an iffy old job, so that cuts out the real pros. They only deal in well rung motors.' Lol considered. 'Probably one of the lock-up lads.' Lol looked at Ray, his face bland as a cabbage. Ray knew the look. He slid twenty quid across the table.

'Buy yourself some bait.'

Lol flashed his car salesman's smile and did a disappearing trick with the grease.

'Let's see, yeah, try . . .' he began.

Dave's car, a battered old 'E' type with patches of grey filler all over it, pulled up outside a backstreet lock-up. Ray and Dave got out. The garage door was open. Inside, a face dressed in oil-caked overalls was working on a stock car. The car was exotically, and very badly, painted, with a huge pair of skin-pink tits on one side. The face was welding a rollbar in position, sparks of molten metal flying from the torch. Ray walked past him into the premises to have a look. He lowered the welding visor and turned to Ray.

'You want something?'

Dave stepped forward. 'I hear you might have some spares for the "E" type.' He indicated his car.

'Where did you hear that from?'

'Lol.'

The face knew the name. He looked Ray and Dave over, not sure of them. 'Don't know where he got that from,' he said uncertainly. 'Don't see many of them around now.'

Ray found a cellulose spray unit. He picked up the gun.

'Do much respraying?' he asked.

'Put that down.'

Ray felt the nozzle. It hadn't been used recently. He gave the face a very hard look and didn't put it down.

'It's busted.' The face swallowed. 'Been busted for weeks; poxy compressor.'

Ray put down the spray gun. He walked back to Dave, who shook his head slightly to say this wasn't the place. They turned to leave and Ray pointed to the stock car.

'You race this?'

'On and off.'

'Win?'

'Now and then.'

Dave and Ray walked out of the garage. The face watched suspiciously as they got into the old 'E' type and drove off. He dropped his visor and went back to his welding.

Lee drove his van off the road on to waste ground overlooking the sea, miles away from anywhere. He pulled the van up and switched off the engine. He lit a cigarette, checked his watch and settled back to wait.

Ray and Dave walked into the body shop. Another face was respraying a Ford Escort. The compressor pumped away, the air was hazed with cellulose. The face looked up. He stopped work and removed the protective mask.

'Help you gents?'

'Got an "E" type outside,' Dave said. 'Needs a blow over.'

'Let's take a look.' He laid down the spray gun and they walked to the door.

'It's been filled, rubbed down,' Dave told him as they went out.

Ray stayed inside to have a quick look round. There was a small office. Ray nipped in and gave it the once over. Nothing. He heard Dave and the face coming back and slipped out to take up his former position by the door.

'How much?' Dave was asking.

'Cash?'

'Sure.'

'Say . . . forty-five?'

They walked back inside. Dave glanced at Ray, who shook his head.

'You supply the paint. I can't take it for a week, I'm booked up,' the face said.

'I'll bell yer.' Dave sounded undecided.

'Suit yourself. You won't find anyone cheaper, not round here.'

The face was a bit miffed at Dave's reluctance to book his car in right away. He went back to work, pulling on the mask and picking up the gun. Dave and Ray walked out.

Lee chain-smoked and lazily watched the boats far out on the horizon. The stillness was broken by a sudden movement at the side of the van.

'You're nicked!'

Lee jumped. He relaxed when he saw who it was.

'You dummy! What you do that for?'

'Testing your reflexes.' The connection laughed. He slid open the passenger door and got in.

'I ought to bust your beak!' Lee clenched his fist.

The connection was younger than Lee, about nineteen and as thin as a stick. He was an obvious head, with an explosion of curly hair, National Health bins and a bum fluff beard. He carried an old army haversack with a Red Cross symbol painted on it.

'How much you got to spend?' he asked.

'Three hundred.'

'What have you been up to?' It was more than he'd expected.

'Bob a job.' Lee smiled.

The connection opened his haversack and took out some pill containers. Then some hash wrapped in silver foil. Lastly, he took out a packet of coke.

'Upwards, downwards or sideways?' he asked.

Dave's 'E' type stopped outside Easy's lock-up. Ray and Dave got out, went to the garage door. It was locked.

'Try round the back,' Ray suggested.

They moved round the side of the garage and found another door. It was locked too. There was a window, high up.

'Give us a lift, Dave.'

Ray got up on Dave's shoulders. He wiped clear a space in the grime and looked in. He saw Kenny's car, resprayed and polished, with rung plates, ready to go out.

'Gotcha!' Ray said.

EIGHTEEN

EASY unlocked the door of the garage. He bolted it behind him and put the take-away coffee and sandwiches down on a bench. He unwrapped the sandwiches, put one in his mouth and walked across to the telephone, coffee in his hand. He put the coffee down, picked up the receiver and dialled.

Still eating, he spoke into the phone.

'Stan, it's Easy. Yeah, it's ready . . . yeah, all done.' He glanced at the car. 'That mustardy yellow. When you coming to collect it?' There was a pause. 'I'm eating a bacon sarni . . . That better?' He swallowed. 'Right . . . yeah. No . . . that's favourite.'

He dropped the receiver, took another bite from his sandwich and picked up the coffee. He turned straight into Ray. He nearly jumped out of his skin. The coffee splashed all over his feet.

'You dropped your coffee,' Ray said.

'Who are you?'

Ray didn't answer the question. 'You got a shake on,' he said.

'How did you – how long have you . . .?'

Ray took the sarni from Easy's fingers. 'Don't talk with yer mouth full.' Ray threw it across the garage. 'It's bad manners.'

Ray moved across to the car, ran his hand appreciatively over the new paint job.

'Nice job,' he said.

'Who are you?'

'Tasty finish,' Ray went on. He saw Easy was edging towards a bench with a panel beating hammer on it.

'You even think about it, I'll gut you!'

Easy stepped away from the bench smartly.

'You better get out of here.' The threat wasn't very convincing.

'Oh, really?'

'What d'you want?'

'The motor. I've come for the motor.'

'Who sent you?' Easy was confused.

'Stan?'

'Stan never sent you.'

'Who's Stan?' Ray asked deadpan.

'You better get lost before he gets here,' Easy tried again.

'Hard man, is he?'

'That's right.'

'Bit of an 'andful?'

'He'll take you.' Easy sounded hopeful.

'You didn't answer my question. Who's Stan?'

Easy made no attempt to reply.

'Who's Rita?' Ray asked patiently.

'Rita?' Easy's pock-marked face registered alarm.

'Rita, Rita,' Ray repeated. 'A real lady. Y'know, the sort who thinks coq au vin is a bunk up in the back of a lorry.'

'I don't know what you're talking about.'

Ray took a coin from his pocket and dragged a long scratch across the bonnet of Kenny's car, exposing the original colour through the respray.

'I'm talkin' about this motor. I'm talkin' about this *stolen* motor. I'm talkin' about the blow job who ripped this motor.'

Easy made a dash for the door, ramming back the bolt and pushing it open. Dave was standing outside and punched him back inside. Ray grabbed him by the neck and hammered his face into the door. He spun him round. Easy's nose was bleeding and his eye was starting to swell already. Ray clamped a hand round Easy's jaw and dug the ends of his fingers into the face muscles.

'Who's Stan?'

Easy couldn't speak for the hold. Ray let go.

'I didn't know the car was stolen,' Easy gasped.

Ray hammered him back against the door.

'Don't . . . tell . . . fibs.' He punctuated each word with a bang against the door.

'Let's try again.' Ray held him up. 'Who's Stan?'

'He knocks cars out . . . front man . . . sells them.'

'Rita?'

Easy didn't answer. Ray hammered him again.

'Ri . . . ta?'

'She's the girlfriend of the face who delivered the car,' Easy got out, breathing heavily.

'His name?'

'Lee.'

'Lee Smith or Smith Lee?'

'Lee Davis.'

'Who is he?'

Easy took a breath. 'He's a nobody, a head, a street dealer.

Flogs pills to kids in the clubs and discos. He's a lump, a big mouth, always bummin' his chat.'

'Where do I find them?'

'I don't know about *him* . . .'

Ray hammered him again.

'*She's* got a place at the back of town.'

'Where?'

'Colfield Street. Thirty-two A.'

Ray glanced at Dave. He nodded, knew where it was.

'You bin there?' Ray asked Easy.

'Yeh.'

'She on the bash?'

'When she's skint.'

Ray clicked his fingers.

'Keys,' he said.

Easy fumbled in his pocket, got them out. Ray grabbed them.

'If I don't find them, or if you're lyin' to me, or if you try to mark their card, I'm goin' to come back, understand?'

Easy nodded.

'Open them doors,' Ray said.

Dave moved quickly outside. Ray got in the car. Easy opened the double doors of the garage and Ray drove out, deliberately just missing him.

'When I read about Kenny I came straight down,' Anna said, opening the door of her flat as Phil walked in.

'He's back.'

'Is he all right?'

They moved down the hallway, into the sitting room.

'He will be.'

'What happened?'

Phil gave the authorised family version of the story. 'He went down to the coast . . . got drunk. Someone stole his car.'

'Oh no.'

'Billy and Vin went down to pick him up.'

Anna kissed Phil. 'Have the family forgiven you? For not going to the fight?'

'Most of them.'

'Billy?'

'Not quite.' They sat down together on the sofa. Phil looked at her. 'I know it's irrational, but I keep thinking if I'd been there, it wouldn't have happened. None of it would have happened.'

'That's not just irrational, it's bloody stupid.' Anna leaned forward and kissed him again.

'What's Kenny going to do? Will he go on boxing?'

'Billy nearly tore my tongue out when I said he might not want to.'

'You don't think he will?'

'It's a decision only Kenny can make.'

'Is it?' Anna asked.

'What do you mean?'

Anna watched Phil closely when she spoke. 'It's not just Kenny in the ring, is it? I mean, from what you've told me, meeting Billy, what he said, it's the whole family. When he's boxing, Kenny *is* the Fox family . . . that's a frightening responsibility.'

Ray forced open the door of Rita's flat and Dave followed him in. They looked cautiously around. Carrier bags had been flung on the unmade bed among piles of new magazines and record albums.

'Looks like she's been spending,' Ray said.

Ray sniffed, sniffed again. He looked at Dave. The room stank of dope. Dave picked a fat roach out of the ashtray by the bed and held it up.

'Twenty-eight skinner,' he said.

'They ain't been gone too long.' Ray found a number of instamatic photos of Rita and Lee stuck round a mirror. He took one, passed it to Dave.

'This must be our hero. Know him?'

Dave checked the face and shook his head. Then Ray saw Kenny's wallet lying open. He picked it up.

'Kenny's wallet.' He waved it at Dave and put it in his pocket.

'What we goin' ter do?' Dave asked. 'Wait for 'em?'

'He's a dealer?'

'Yeah?'

Ray thought. 'Clubs and discos, the man said. He's probably used the dough to score some stock. He's goin' to be out hustling.'

Rita, dressed to kill, was dancing with Lee. The disco had megawatt music to go with the strobes, low lights and bopping bodies. Lee was still wearing Kenny's jacket. They'd been drinking and smoking and they were well laid back.

A kid of fifteen approached Lee. Lee left Rita dancing by herself, hardly noticing he'd gone, and made his way with the kid to the men's lavatories. Inside, they waited until another kid left. The kid handed Lee thirty quid. Lee passed him an envelope made into a small package with sellotape and headed for the door. The kid stayed behind. He opened one end of the package and checked the pills inside. He seemed satisfied, popped two and washed them down with a quarter bottle of cheap scotch he took from his pocket.

Billy heard some movement in Kenny's room and looked in. The boy seemed to have made a good recovery. A hot bath, good food and plenty of sleep had worked wonders. Billy came in. Kenny had an open suitcase on the bed. He'd piled in everything he could find in his room to remind him of his boxing. Amateur cups and medals, photographs, his ring kit. It was all there.

'I thought I heard you movin' around. What are you doin', son?'

Kenny just looked at him.

'Oh . . . good,' Billy said sarcastically, when he realised.

'Don't . . . don't, Pop. Please.'

'Don't what?'

'Make it harder than it is.'

Billy sat on the bed. Kenny finished packing the case.

'It won't change a thing, Kenny. It won't bring Charlie Locke back.'

'It just might help me live with it,' Kenny said.

'She didn't mean what she said, Kenny, Charlie's wife. She was drunk.'

'I'm goin' to send her some money. I've got three thousand in the Building Society.'

'She phoned your mum while we was at the coast. She wanted to come and see you, say she was sorry.'

'She's sorry!' Kenny said in wonder. 'I killed her husband and *she* wants to apologise to *me*!'

'Let her talk to you, Kenny. For her sake as much as yours, maybe more. In a day or so, when you're feelin' more up to it.'

'She won't change my mind. It's finished, over. I ain't goin' to fight again – ever.'

'What about Eddie?'

'Eddie's got other fighters.'

'Not like you he hasn't.'

'He'll find one.'

'You know that's not true. Prospects like you, son, only come along once in a lifetime for the Eddies of this world. You'll break his heart.'

'I can't help it,' Kenny cried out. 'I can't help how I *feel.* I wouldn't be no use to him *now*. It's gone. Up here!' He tapped his head. 'Eddie's always sayin' it's up here where fights are won. That's the difference between a champion and an undercard fighter. It's gone, Pop. Every time I'd climb into a ring I'd see Charlie Locke.'

Kenny sat on the bed next to Billy. He was still a bit wobbly. 'I can still feel that punch . . . see the gumshield go!' He spoke quietly now. 'Charlie was on the deck, shakin'. I remember seein' a dog run over when I was a kid; it was dead but it was still movin'. I can still see Charlie's face on that stretcher. I won't ever forget that face.'

Tears slipped down Kenny's cheeks. Billy put his arms round his youngest son and cuddled him as if he were a frightened child. Kenny sobbed, the emotion of the past few days pouring out of him.

It took some time to track them down, but Dave knew the disco scene pretty well. Lee and Rita were having a ball, dancing themselves into the ground at another disco. Dave sat in the shadows, watching every move they made. A young bird he'd met came up.

'Thought it was you,' she said.

Dave looked up briefly, said nothing.

'By y'self?'

'No.' Dave's eyes went back to the dance floor.

'Oh. Didn't think you liked places like this?'

'I don't.' Dave hoped she'd shove off, but she didn't.

'What you here for then? You're not with no one, are you?'

She went to sit beside him. Dave took her wrist and squeezed.

'Not tonight darlin'.'

'You're 'urting!'

Dave released his grip, leaving white fingermarks on her wrist and arm.

'Get lost!' he said.

The bird moved back into the disco crowd, rubbing her wrist resentfully. Dave settled back to watch Lee and Rita, who had gone into a very rude clinch in the middle of the dance floor.

Outside the club, Lee's van was parked close to Dave's 'E' type. Lee and Rita came out of the disco. Dave was just behind them and quickly got into his car.

Lee and Rita slid open the van doors and got in. Lee leaned over and grabbed Rita, running his hand over her body as he kissed her. She was enjoying it, but Lee froze as a gun was pushed into the back of his neck. Ray's voice came from the back of the van.

'One dodgy move, lover, and you're goin' to swallow this shooter!'

The van drove through the seaside town, followed by the 'E' type. Both cars entered the drive of the derelict house. Rita and Lee got out; Ray was behind them with the gun. Dave joined them, carrying a torch.

'You can have the money back,' Lee pleaded. His sphincter had gone completely. 'I've got the money . . . I've got more.' He started pulling the money from his dealing in the discos out of his pocket.

'You can have it all,' Lee said, turning to Rita. 'She's got money, show him.'

Rita took nearly a hundred from her trouser pocket, showed it to Ray.

'A hundred – take it.' She tried to push the money on Ray, but he slapped it out of her hand and pointed the gun at them.

'You want to die here?'

Lee was shaking with fear.

'We didn't know who he was . . . we didn't know about *you*!'

'Get in the house,' Ray ordered.

Dave led them down the passage to the cellar. Ray followed with the gun. At the door they stopped.

'In,' said Ray.

'Please, please, don't kill us,' Lee begged.

'It was his idea, not mine,' Rita screamed. 'I didn't want to do it.'

'*Get in* there!' Ray said harshly.

Lee and Rita went into the cellar. Dave held the torch on their faces, blinding them. They were sure they were going to die.

'I was worried about Kenny,' Rita said desperately. 'He'll tell you. Covered him up, look . . . look . . . with this.' She picked up the damp curtain, still on the chair. 'I covered him up,' she begged.

'What did you feed him?'

'What?'

'You doped him?'

'Nembutal,' Lee said. He took a bottle of downers from his pocket.

'How many?'

'I can't . . . can't . . .' Lee was shaking.

'*How many?*'

'Three. Three.'

'Take three each.' Ray's voice was menacing. They still couldn't see because of the torch in their eyes. They didn't understand. Ray snatched the bottle from Lee and threw it to Dave.

'Give 'em three each,' he said.

Dave uncorked the bottle and took out six nembutal. He gave them three each. They had trouble getting them down.

'Show me. Open your mouth.'

They opened their mouths and Ray checked they'd swallowed the pills.

'Right . . . now strip off,' he said.

Lee and Rita looked at each other uncomprehendingly.

'Get yer clothes *off*!'

Rita started to cry. Lee was shaking so badly he could hardly stand. They slowly stripped off. Rita stopped at her pants.

'Don't tell me you're embarrassed, you garbage!' Ray shouted at her.

Rita took off her pants. She stood close to Lee, the two of them looking totally vulnerable and terrified in their nakedness. Dave collected up their clothes, backed out of the door and passed Ray the torch. Ray held the torch on them and raised the gun as if to blow them away. They cowered against the wall, trying to hide behind one another as though they were facing a firing squad. Ray cut the torch and slammed the door, leaving them in darkness.

*

Outside, Dave threw the clobber in the back of the van.

'You take my motor, pick Kenny's up. I'll dump this heap,' he said.

Ray had the money from Lee and Rita. He counted off Billy's five hundred. There was one eighty left. He handed it to Dave.

'This is one I owe you, Dave. Any time you need me, you know where I am.'

Dave took the money. 'What about them?'

'I'd like to let them rot down there. Better let 'em out tomorrow night.'

Dave smiled. 'It's goin' to be a bit parky.'

Ray nodded. 'I'm sure they'll find a way of keepin' warm.'

Dave offered his hand, Ray shook it.

'Stay lucky, eh?' Dave said.

It was the middle of the night when Ray drove Kenny's car out on the London road. Kenny's jacket, boots and wallet were on the passenger seat. For the first time Ray seemed relaxed, smoking a cigarette and driving with one hand. The cat's-eyes winked in the headlights as the car powered along the pitch-black road. Ray began to laugh as he thought back over the scene in the derelict house. He went on laughing for quite a while.

NINETEEN

A BIG black limousine raced through the university grounds. A side window was cracked, there were kick marks down both sides of the limo and it was splattered with paint. In the front, Rushmer, a student from the University Conservative Association, was explaining the quickest route across the internal road system to the uniformed driver. In the back, Leeson, a nationally known politician, was supported by one of his aides while the other held a white towel to his head. The towel was red with blood still flowing from a serious head wound.

The driver hammered the car round a corner of the one way system, nearly running down two students. He blasted the horn angrily and Rushmer frantically waved the students to one side. The driver saw the front gates ahead and accelerated fast towards them. Rushmer, at his side, indicated which way to turn.

Kenny, well oiled, was sunbathing beside a hotel pool in Spain. Nan was sitting near him at an umbrella table, writing postcards home. They both had good suntans and looked very relaxed. Kenny was almost asleep.

'What do I say to Eddie?' Nan asked.

'Wha . . .?' Kenny dozed.

'Eddie . . . I'm doing Eddie's card. You want to say anything special?'

'Special?'

'His letter . . . about the letter he sent you?'

Kenny got up on his elbow. 'Tell 'im, say . . .' Kenny considered. 'What the 'ell do I say to him?'

'That you'll see him when you get back,' Nan suggested.

'Even then?' Kenny was doubtful.

'He thinks you're going to change your mind.'

Kenny sighed. 'I know.'

'He thinks a month in the sun will do it.'

'Then he'll have to think again.'

'Poor Eddie,' Nan said. 'I thought he was going to cry when you told him you wouldn't fight again.'

'That's a day I'd rather forget.'

'Billy thinks so, too . . .' Nan was off in her own thoughts.

'That I'll change my mind?'

'That all you needed was a long holiday.'

'He knows me better than that.' Kenny sounded a little unsure.

'That wasn't what he said when I heard him arguing with Phil.'

'Can't we talk about something else, please. Better still, you get on with your cards – "Havin' a lovely time, wish you was 'ere" – and let me go rusty.'

Nan wasn't offended. She turned back to her cards and pretended to write, correcting Kenny's grammar.

'Having . . . a . . . lovely . . . time . . . wish . . . you . . . *were* . . . here,' she said out loud.

Kenny smiled. 'Naughty,' he said and settled back on his sun bed.

Gadsden was one of the senior administrators of the university, a thin-faced, tight-lipped man in his early fifties. Phil had never got on with him in their few encounters. Phil looked across the methodically ordered desk and waited.

'I have a complete list of the individuals involved,' Gadsden said. He fingered a piece of paper in front of him on the desk.

'Do you?' Phil was non-committal.

'Would you care to see it?' Gadsden picked it up as if to threaten Phil with it.

'No, thank you.'

There was a long silence. They sized each other up. 'Responsibility,' Gadsden said at last. 'At some point someone has to take responsibility. In situations like this the question of responsibility must arise.'

Phil said nothing. 'A guest of this university, an eminent invited guest, has been attacked.' Gadsden paused for effect. 'Maliciously assaulted, injured. Badly injured by a student of this university.'

'And you consider that is my responsibility?' Phil asked quietly.

'You organised the demonstration.'

'I didn't organise Mr Leeson's visit. Alan Rushmer . . . the University Conservative Association did that.'

'What has that to do with it?' Gadsden asked coldly.

'Where does their responsibilty lie? The UCA must have known that bringing a man like Leeson into any university in this country to debate race relations would without question *provoke* demonstration. Leeson is one of the most dangerous men in national politics, a self-confessed racist.'

Gadsden put down the piece of paper. 'This is an academic institution in one of the few real democracies left. As such it cannot and should not commit itself to hold any particular moral or political view.'

'What a stimulating definition of democracy,' Phil said caustically.

'We are not here to argue political philosophy.' Gadsden tried to stare him down but Phil held his gaze.

'We have over three hundred black undergraduates here. What did the UCA expect them to do?'

'Certainly not behave like thugs,' Gadsden replied quickly.

'You saw the incident?'

'Of course not.'

'Then how do you know how we behaved? Or how the UCA behaved? Or how Leeson's lackeys conducted themselves?'

'I have several reports.'

'Who from?'

'People who were present. Eye witnesses.'

'Names?' Phil asked.

'I cannot say at the moment.'

'Can't or won't?'

'This is a police matter.'

'Then I'll tell you. Rushmer, Leal, Melrose?' Phil looked at Gadsden for confirmation but he didn't get a flicker. 'What a triumvirate, the last of the dodos. Why don't you get Rushmer back here now, with me, and we'll try to sort out the truth?'

'As I said, this is now a police matter.' Gadsden was ice.

'Perhaps they will be less prejudiced.'

Gadsden shrugged. 'No doubt they will be in contact with you. Pending a more thorough investigation of the facts, you will be instructed to appear before a disciplinary committee.'

'You don't really want to know what happened, do you? All you want is a body.'

Gadsden's tone became bland. 'My concern is to protect the high reputation of this university. If you insist on organising violent demonstrations you must, I am afraid, accept the inevitable consequences.'

Phil was losing his resolution to keep his temper. 'All this cant about responsibility. You're not interested in moral accountability, you just want a skin to nail to the fence, preferably white, preferably radical. The "fascist left", what could be more logical or convenient, the ideal victim.'

'That is an invidious imputation.'

'The perfect scapegoat syndrome,' Phil said angrily. 'Whoever is guilty is punished, therefore whoever is punished is guilty and whoever is not punished is not guilty. The condemnation of another constitutes the acquittal of oneself.'

A group of friends gathered in Phil's room to discuss what had happened. Don, Femi and Rast were there, all a few years younger than Phil. Feelings were running high about Gadsden's action.

'He can't do that—' Don was saying.

'He has!' Femi said.

'That's victimisation.' Rast banged his fist against the wall in frustration.

'He'll have to put us *all* in front of the committee,' Don said. 'Did Gadsden give you a date for this hearing?'

'No,' Phil said quietly.

'We'll find out when it is.'

'Occupy the building,' Rast suggested quickly.

'This time it won't be thirty,' Femi promised. 'It'll be three hundred.'

'Those bastards aren't going to get away with this.' Don spoke for them all.

'I'm sorry, no. You've got it all wrong,' Phil said, looking round at them.

'What?' Don didn't understand.

'You're thinking too obviously . . . demos, confrontations. Think instead, all those academic anachronisms in one room at the same time!'

Don was amazed. 'You *want* to come up in front of that committee?'

'I don't want you to prevent it. Do you understand?'

They all looked blank.

'Perhaps, just perhaps, I could convince them that to demonstrate against Leeson was the right thing to do.'

Rast objected. 'And perhaps, just perhaps, they'll crucify you.'

'That's a risk I'll take.'
'They'll boot you out, Phil!' Don warned.
'*Then* you can do what you want.'

Phil and Anna walked through the university grounds. 'I'm going to go away for a few days,' Phil said. 'Let things calm down.'

Anna said nothing.

'Can I use your place?'

She took her flat keys from her bag and passed them to Phil.

'Thanks. What about you?'

'I thought you'd want to be alone.' She looked at him appraisingly. 'To prepare yourself spiritually for your historic confrontation with the forces of darkness,' she said mockingly.

'I know what I'm doing, Anna.'

'You think you do. But you're underestimating the system.'

'Maybe.'

'Listen to me, Phil, I grew up among people like Gadsden. They always win, somehow.'

'Like your father.' Phil knew this was hitting below the belt.

'Yes,' Anna said, '*just* like my father.'

Joey and Griff had met up by chance at a cab rank in town and Griff had parked his hack behind Joey's.

Joey was sitting on the luggage step of his cab with a postcard from Kenny and Nan in Spain, while Griff leaned back on the cab eating an ice-cream cone.

'Kenny says to tell you the hotel's full of choice birds.' Joey looked up from the card. 'German, French, Scandinavian . . .'

Griff poked his ice-cream cone up suggestively. 'Whhheeeeee.'

Joey continued to read. 'He says if you were here it'd be like a poacher's dog in a pheasant farm.'

'Not many,' Griff laughed. 'Whoaaa . . . get 'em down, senorita! Ooooooh . . . you're brown *all over*!'

'We miss you a lot,' Joey read. 'Love Nan . . . PS Have you . . .' Joey stopped.

'Have you what?' Griff asked.

'Private.'

Griff grabbed the postcard and read.

'PS Have you seen Bette recently?'

Joey snatched it back. 'Nose!' he said indignantly.

'Have you?' Griff asked.

'Na . . .' Joey said dismissively.

'I thought you was in love?'

'She's a freak.'

'What happened?'

'Nothing happened.'

'*Something* happened.' Griff was sure of it.

Joey pointed to his mouth. ' 'Ere, watch my lips. Noth . . . ing . . . hap . . . pened. She just weren't my type.'

'Randy, rude and rich. Not your type – you better shape up, my son.'

Joey deliberately jogged Griff's elbow as he was eating his cornet and the ice-cream squidged up Griff's nose.

Billy and Connie drove round to Vin's house to discuss Andy's future. Vin and Renie had taken him for a series of tests at a special school for deaf kids outside London. They'd been very impressed with the place. The teaching standards were high and the facilities were much better than anything they'd seen before. Now they had to wait for the results of the tests. Renie was really excited.

'If he's accepted, he can be educated there until he's seventeen,' she told Billy.

'How far is it exactly, Vin?' Billy asked.

'A hundred and forty somethin' the round trip. 'Bout seventy, seventy-five.'

'He'd have to board,' Renie said.

Connie was unsure. 'He's a bit young for that, isn't he?'

'He'd come home most weekends,' Vin said quickly.

'The girls'll miss him,' Billy said.

'What he means is he'll miss him,' Connie explained.

Billy frowned. 'We *all* will.'

'There's nowhere closer . . .' Renie was anxious Billy should approve.

'. . . that's as good, anyway,' Vin added.

Connie was coming round to the idea. 'It does sound marvellous.'

'All the kids seemed so happy,' Vin said.

'Andy loved it, you could tell,' Renie appealed to Billy.

'If it's the *best*, that's what we want for him,' Billy said at last. 'The best, he deserves it.'

'They all do, poor little mites,' Connie said. 'There should be schools as good as this one all over the country, not just here and there. People just don't know, maybe they don't want to know . . . someone ought to cause a stink about it.'

'You tell 'em, gel,' Billy said approvingly.

'It makes me cross.'

'We've got to be sensible,' Vin warned. 'I mean, he's not there yet.'

'He's as good as in. One look at that kid's face and they melt like butter.'

'You could be slightly biased, Billy,' Connie said.

Billy smiled. 'He's a Fox, ain't he?'

'I hope you're right, Billy. I do hope you're right,' Renie joked.

'I ain't bein' a misery,' Vin said. 'I just don't want to get all our hopes up too high.'

Phil made his way through the apartment block to Anna's flat. He took the keys from his pocket and let himself in. He walked, deep in thought, down the hallway into the sitting room and came face to face with Anna's mother. She stood at the drinks cabinet hastily putting away a brandy bottle and a used balloon glass. When she saw it was Phil she just stood there, looking at him.

'I'm, I'm sorry. Anna didn't tell me that you . . .' Phil stumbled over his apology.

'Is Anna with you?' She closed the cabinet with a bang.

'No, no, she isn't.'

A moment of relief showed on her face. She moved away from the cabinet abruptly, as though to dissociate herself from it.

'Sometimes, when I'm in town, I come here. London seems to be so . . . so noisy now. So manic . . . exhausting.'

Phil realised she was quite drunk. She looked tired and drawn, though she was still impeccably dressed.

'It's peaceful here, cool,' she went on. Phil noticed she wasn't wearing her shoes. She moved back to the chair she'd been sitting in before he came in. Her shoes were there, next to two Harrods carrier-bags.

'To be alone, quite alone for a few moments. For me that's . . .

that's quite a luxury.'

She went to slip her shoes on, but one of them fell over. She had difficulty in getting it upright again and on her foot.

'I can come back later?' Phil was embarrassed. More than she appeared to be.

'No . . . no. No, I was about to leave.'

She got the shoes on, picked up the Harrods bags and immediately dropped one. Phil moved over, picked it up for her.

'Thank you.' She started to walk to the door, slowly and deliberately. 'I would prefer that Anna didn't know I was here. It's Anna's flat. I don't want her to think that I . . .' She steadied herself by holding on to the door handle.

'Of course,' Phil said.

'It's Philip, isn't it?'

'Yes.'

'Philip . . .' she repeated.

Phil followed her out into the hallway. At the front she dropped one of the bags again. She stumbled as she leaned down to retrieve it. Phil took her arm to help her but she snatched it away.

'Don't touch me!' She glared at him.

Phil backed away. Anna's mother left the Harrods bag on the floor, moved to the door, opened it and walked out. She slammed the door shut behind her.

TWENTY

RAY was in his office, shaving with a cordless razor. There was a tap at the door. 'It's open,' he called.

Ray went on shaving when Madeline came in.

'You're early.'

'I wanted to see you.'

'What about?' Ray switched off the razor. 'If it's about money, sweet'eart, I'm sorry but I can't . . .'

'It's not,' Madeline said quickly.

'I've 'ad the piano tuned, so it can't be that?' Ray said lightly.

She looked straight at him. 'Alan and me, we don't live together.'

'Look, love, your private life is *private*, none of my business.'

She kept her eyes on his. 'But I want it to be.'

'I don't think Alan would go a million on that,' he said quietly.

She shrugged. 'I've known him for years. It's never been serious.'

'I've seen the way he looks at you.'

'I've seen the way *you* look at me,' Madeline said.

Phil sat in Anna's flat, watching the news on television. The front doorbell rang. He turned down the volume and went to see who it was.

'Pop!' It was the last person he expected.

'Anna told me where you was.'

Phil could see at a glance that something was very wrong.

'What's up?'

Billy came in. They walked through to the sitting room.

'The local law have been round to the house. They wanted to know where you were.'

'Why?'

'The Birmingham police have been on to them, asked them to check you out.'

'What did they want?'

'You know bloody well what they wanted,' Billy told him tersely.

Phil crossed to the television set and switched it off. 'I was going to ring you.'

'When?'

'Tomorrow.'

'You've been here three days?'

'It's been . . . difficult,' Phil stalled.

'To pick up a phone to call your *family*. Difficult?'

'I needed some time alone to think things out.'

'What's gone wrong with you, son? I don't recognise you no more. I don't understand you. None of us do. Ain't we had enough to worry about with Kenny? It's almost like you do these things on purpose.'

Phil didn't know how to answer him. 'What did they tell you?'

Billy shook his head wearily. 'The local boys nothin' . . . they weren't told nothin', 'cept to check on you. I rang Birmingham. They told me you're bang in bother.'

Phil looked puzzled. 'Why, because I came down here?'

'He's got eight stitches in his 'ead!' Billy shouted. 'A bloody MP!'

'I had nothing to do with that.'

'Don't you lie to me, Phil. Don't you start that. You ain't never lied to me before.'

'I'm not lying to you now.' Phil couldn't understand why his father was so strung up. 'I didn't throw that bottle.'

'They say you did,' Billy said flatly.

'What?'

'They say they've got a witness that saw you. Positive. Identified you – a written statement.'

Phil just couldn't believe it. 'A student?'

'No, not a student.'

'*Who* then?'

'They didn't say, but they were bloody sure of themselves. I told them I didn't know where you was. I didn't, not till I rung Anna.'

'Did she know about this?'

Billy misunderstood him. 'She was with you, wasn't she, at this bloody riot?'

'No, I mean about the witness – this statement?'

'I didn't ask her,' Billy said. 'I just wanted to know where to find you. Look, son, no matter what you've done, what trouble you're in, we're your family. We want to help. How the bloody 'ell can we if you treat us like strangers?'

'What are you talking about?'

Billy gestured extravagantly round the expensively furnished room. 'This. Is this your home now?'

'That's an evil thing to say, Pop.'

Billy wasn't deterred. 'Is this what you're about? Don't fit too well with your politics, do it, boy? All them books you read, lectures you got to? All them arguments you have with Vinnie?'

Billy looked round the room to take it all in. 'I thought your lot hated all this? I thought grand pianos and Persian carpets was "the trappings of the bourgeois". I thought this is what the revolution is goin' ter do away with? Or is it all talk with your lot?'

Billy took a breath before going on. 'You slag Vinnie off who's bustin' his balls to make a livin', and 'ere you are cased up with a sort who ain't never 'ad to clean 'er own shoes. I bet her old man dodges more taxes than all your family earns put together.'

Billy pointed round the flat. 'How much is this posh 'ole worth? Probably more money than I made all me life. You're a ponce, the worst sort. A hypocritical ponce!'

'You're talking a load of rubbish!' Phil retorted.

'I thought you was supposed to be the smart one. All yer teachers used to tell us what a clever little devil you was. Jack the Lad, and we was so proud of you, all of us.' Billy paused. 'Well I ain't so proud of you now. I ain't proud of what you've become, what you're involved in. I ain't proud of having the law bangin' on my door lookin' for yer. Or on the phone tellin' me an' yer mother what a dangerous little bastard you are!'

' "A likely candidate for an outrage",' Phil quoted. 'You're just like the rest, all you want to do is accuse, point the finger, shout and scream. You'd rather believe what they tell you than listen to me.'

'I've bin listening to you ever since you went to that place. You're supposed to be a "mature student", that much older than the rest of 'em. That's rich, you're behaving like a bloody three-year-old.' Billy laughed harshly. He'd been waiting a long time to have it all out with Phil and nothing was going to stop him now.

'I've watched you change,' he said. 'I've tried to understand, made excuses when you didn't turn up, when we knew you was in London, never phoned. What is it, boy? Are we too common for you now, too pig-ignorant, do we embarrass you? Is that what it's all come down to? Is that what education means?'

'I think you've said enough, Pop,' Phil said sadly.

'Don't you call me that,' Billy said emotionally. 'I ain't Pop to you no more. Your mother cried her eyes out.'

This upset Phil more than Billy's insults.

'I'm . . . I'm sorry about that.'

'You're always sorry these days, ain't yer?' Billy said quickly. 'That word comes very easy to you. You was *sorry* when you couldn't get home last Christmas. You was *sorry* about the shout up you had with Vin, all them snide things you called him. You was *sorry* about missin' Kenny's fight. Now you're *sorry* again. Well, I don't believe you no more. I don't think you're sorry, I think you're a selfish lyin' little swine!'

Billy turned to go. Phil was stunned by his father's outburst but he reached out and put a hand on his shoulder to turn him back.

'Pop—'

Billy turned, his fist raised.

'Go on, if it'll make you feel better.'

Billy stood with his fist ready to hit Phil.

'Go on!'

Billy slowly lowered his hand.

'That's the way you've been solving your problems for fifty years, why stop now?'

Billy turned to leave again. Phil followed.

'King Billy! Anything you don't agree with, anything you don't understand . . .' Phil clenched a fist and punched it into the palm of his other hand. 'Do it to him before he does it to you! I was five when you taught me that, my first day at school.'

Billy walked out of the sitting room. Phil followed him into the hall, angry at his father's strained silence.

'You *are* ignorant! You're a narrow-minded, obsessive old man, living in the past. All you've got in your heart and head is the *family*, the great Fox family . . .'

Billy opened the front door, stood there looking at Phil.

'King Billy's boys! You're going to die one day. What happens then? What happens to the Fox dynasty then?'

Billy looked at his son disdainfully.

'You know what?' Phil finished. 'When you die, we'll all be able to breathe. Vin, Ray, Joey, Kenny, me . . . we'll be able to live our own lives when you're gone!'

Billy went out and slammed the door behind him. Phil pressed his face against the cool wood, instantly wishing he could withdraw the cruel words.

Phil stood in the small CID interview room and waited. A young Detective Sergeant, about the same age as Phil, came in.

'My name's Poyzer,' he said.

'I phoned my father,' Phil lied. 'He said you were looking for me?'

'We were told you'd gone home. The address registered at the university is your parents'.'

'I was at a friend's flat.'

'Why did you leave?' Poyzer asked in a neutral voice.

'I thought maybe things would calm down if I wasn't around for a few days.'

'Didn't Mr Gadsden tell you we wanted to see you?'

'He said something. I can't remember exactly.'

'And so you left, almost immediately.'

'Only for a few days.'

'Nearly four days,' Poyzer corrected.

'I didn't leave deliberately to avoid seeing you. If that were the case, why would I be here now?'

Poyzer took out a pack of cigarettes and lit one. He indicated the table and two chairs. They sat opposite one another.

'My father told me you have a signed statement that I threw the bottle?'

'That's correct.'

'Who from?'

'A workman on the roof overlooking that rear entrance. He was repairing the guttering.'

'And he identified me?' Phil was astonished.

Poyzer took a notebook from his inside pocket and flicked it open. He searched through the pages, found the place and read aloud: 'Jeans. Tan boots. Dark green leather jacket, one of the lapels torn. White disc badge in the other lapel. Multi-coloured striped sweater. Denim shirt . . .'

Poyzer looked up at Phil. Phil couldn't believe what was happening. It was certainly his description.

'I didn't throw that bottle.'

'Why would Mr Lowe come to us, insist you did, give us your description?'

'I have no idea.'

'He was quite sure,' Poyzer said.

'He must be mistaken, or he's lying.'

'Why should he do that? What possible motive could he have for lying?'

Phil was at a complete loss. 'I can't believe this. I just can't believe it. It's like something out of Kafka. Can I speak to him?'

'No.'

'With you present?'

Poyzer shook his head.

'If charges are brought, he'd be the principal prosecution witness.'

Phil didn't understand. '*If* charges are brought?'

'Mr Leeson has requested that our inquiries be dropped.'

'*Leeson* has?'

'He rang through this morning. My guvnor is considering the matter.' Poyzer permitted himself a tight smile. 'Mr Leeson is a man not without influence.'

'And not without a laser instinct for propaganda publicity. Look what the lunatic left have done to me, but I forgive them "for they know not what they do". Leeson's Calvary. It's got to be worth a few votes.'

Phil's little speech irritated Poyzer.

'If I were you, my friend, I'd shut my silly mouth and count myself very lucky. You could have been on a very serious assault with intent charge, malicious wounding. You could've ended up with two years. You still might, so why don't you just shut it!' Poyzer pointed to his mouth. 'And keep it shut!'

When they were seated in front of his desk Mr Cant, the school principal, smiled at Renie and Vin.

'I'm delighted to tell you Andy has been accepted.'

He was a sweet-looking man in his late thirties, scruffy in appearance and dress, with the kind of face that always seemed to be breaking into a smile. They made no attempt to hide their delight.

'Oh . . . thank you!' Renie said.

'That's wonderful.' Vin beamed back at him, then unselfconsciously he leaned over and kissed Renie.

'We'll start him next September,' Cant said. 'I've been on to the ILEA and they are expecting you to contact them about the financial arrangements.'

There was a knock at the door and a beautiful girl of fifteen came in with a tray of tea. She put the tray carefully down on the principal's already cluttered desk. Cant introduced her, making sure she could see his lips.

'This is Suzi. She makes the best tea.'

Suzi blushed and smiled at him.

'Suzi came to us four years ago.' He spoke directly to her. 'Four years you've been here?'

'Nearly . . . five years . . . now.' Her speech was slow and deliberate, but quite coherent. 'This Seep . . . Sept . . . September.'

'This is Mr and Mrs Fox. Their boy is starting school next September.' Cant enunciated each word.

Suzi nodded and turned to leave. Renie reached out and touched her hand. 'Thank you for the tea.'

Suzi smiled at her and went out.

'By the way, where is Andy?' Cant asked.

'His grandad took him fishing.'

'Special treat,' Vin added.

Billy and Andy had found a solitary spot for their fishing, a lake miles from anywhere and surrounded by woods. The boy was a natural angler, his deafness was compensated by a gift for total concentration. Billy watched him, eyes glued to his bobbing float. Suddenly he hooked a fish. Billy came over to help him land it, but Andy was a stubborn, fiercely independent little boy. He insisted on landing it himself. He showed it proudly to Billy, then expertly put it in the keep net.

Renie and Vin felt very happy about their morning at the school. Driving back, Vin pulled the car in at a country pub for a celebratory drink. It was a cosy little place with an easy, relaxed atmosphere. There were only a couple of locals having a late morning drink when they went up to the bar. Archie Wegner stood behind it, a dapper little man in his sixties with silver hair and a waxed moustache.

'Good morning, handsome day,' he greeted them.

'It certainly is,' Vin agreed.

'What's your pleasure?'

Vin turned to Renie.

'Sherry, please . . . sweet.'

'I'll have a small scotch and soda. No ice.'

Wegner turned away to get their drinks. Renie sat on a high stool and looked round the pub.

'This is lovely.'

'We've got plenty of time,' Vin said. 'Pop said they'd be back about five.'

Wegner put the drinks in front of them on mats. 'Little bit quiet this morning.'

'You're the landlord?' Vin asked.

'The owner. It's a free house.'

Vin gave him a pound note. Wegner turned to the till.

'They don't have pubs like this in London,' Renie said.

Wegner handed over Vin's change.

'It's got to be South London?'

'I beg your pardon?' Vin said.

'I can always tell. We've been down here twenty-two years and I can still tell. I was born in New Cross.'

'Never!'

'Snead Street, number fifteen. It's all gone now. We were up there recently, visiting my sister. All gone, it's a park now. Grass, kids playing . . . nice.'

'We're from Battersea,' Renie said.

'Stroll on.' Wegner dropped easily into the vernacular.

'That's more like it,' Vin smiled.

'Maisie,' Wegner called out.

His wife appeared behind her husband, a plump woman with a healthy outdoor complexion.

'This is my wife. These good people are from Battersea.'

'I was born in Lavender Hill.'

'Where?' Renie asked.

'Along the Sweep.'

'Well, I'll be blowed.'

'Small world,' Wegner said.

Vin looked at them almost enviously.

'You both look country born and bred.'

'Twenty-two years ago we moved out, come here,' Maisie said.

Wegner nodded. 'Best day's work we ever did.'

'I couldn't ever go back,' his wife added.

'We like the odd night out in Town.' Wegner smiled at Vin. 'Nice meal with friends, maybe a show. But that's it. That's quite enough for us, then straight back home.'

'It isn't like it used to be, is it?' Maisie looked at Renie. 'I mean, everyone rushing everywhere like the place is on fire.'

Billy stopped fishing to unpack a picnic prepared for them by Connie. He unwrapped sandwiches, hard boiled eggs, apples, chunks of fresh cheese, chocolate biscuits and a flask of sweet tea. He was laying them out, with a bottle of orange for Andy, when a couple of anglers passed by. They carried a load of expensive equipment.

'How's your luck?' the first one asked.

'The nipper's catching 'em all, makin' me look like a donkey.' Billy pointed to Andy, still fiercely concentrating on his line.

'What bait are you using, son?' the angler asked.

Of course Andy didn't hear the question.

'Paste,' Billy answered. 'He puts honey in it.'

'What ground bait?' the second angler asked.

Andy went on fishing, oblivious of the men.

'Breadcrumbs, bran and brown rice,' Billy said.

The angler smiled, pointed to Andy. 'Don't give much away, does he?'

They started to move off.

'Good luck,' Billy called after them.

In the country pub, Wegner and Vin talked while Maisie showed Renie the flower-filled garden at the back.

'We're going to retire in the autumn.' Wegner smiled. 'While we're still young enough to do a spot of travelling. Maisie wants to go and see her brother in New Zealand. We're going through the Med, Egypt, on to India, the grand tour . . . then come back through the States and Canada.'

Vin nodded approvingly. 'What about this place?'

'It's going on the market soon.'

Vin pricked up his ears.

'When?'

'Next month or so, there's no rush.'

Wegner went off to serve one of his regulars. After a few moments he came back, a half pint in his hand.

'Don't mind me asking . . .' Vin said. 'How much would you want for it?'

'Ohhh, that's not easy. It's a good little house. We've made a very comfortable living out of it. And put a fair bit by.'

Vin was very interested. 'It hasn't been advertised yet . . . or put in the hands of an agent?'

'Actually, you're the first person I've really discussed it with. Maisie and me was only talking about it last week. We were going to wait till next year but I said to her, we said that *last* year.'

Driving home, Vin told Renie about his talk with Archie Wegner.

'It's only a few miles from Andy's school, and there's a school for the girls even nearer,' Vin said excitedly. 'I reckon if I could get Wally to buy my share of the firm, what we would get for the house on a quick sale, we've got some saved, and a mortgage . . . we could make an offer *before* it goes on the open market.'

Renie wasn't sure Vin realised what he was committing himself to.

'You're not just saying all this, Vin? I mean, you do realise what you *are* saying.'

'Course I do.'

She went through it. 'Apart from the money side, you're talking about selling the business, the house, moving out of London – a long way out, being separated from the family.'

'I thought you'd be enthusiastic.' Vin was disappointed. 'I thought you'd be leaping about. Ain't this what you've always wanted?'

'Vinnie, Vinnie. Of course it is. It's like something out of a dream. I'm sorry, I didn't mean to throw cold water on it. It's just, it's *you* who's got to be sure. I'd pack up and go tomorrow.'

'I'm sure,' Vin said simply.

'You're not just saying that for me, for Andy, are you?'

'No, love, I ain't and that's the God's honest truth. I'm well gutted with breakin' my back, everyone comin' to me with their moans, workin' fourteen hours a day. An' I want my kids to know something else but the Smoke, while they're still young enough.'

Renie was almost convinced. 'But what about the family . . . Billy?'

'We'll deal with that when we have to. It ain't like goin' to Australia. It's only seventy-five miles away. They can all come down to visit, holidays, maybe even have Christmas in the country.'

'You really reckon we could manage it?'

'It'd be a squeeze. We'd have to borrow, but I do, I really do.'

Vin steered with one hand, put an arm round Renie and gave her a hug.

Andy finished his lunch quickly and got up, making a sign to Billy that he was going back to his fishing. Billy nodded and began to pack away what was left of the food. He leaned down to pick up the flask of tea and a terrible pain scythed through his chest, shocking the breath out of his body. He dropped the flask and fell back, clutching his chest.

Andy had baited his hook, cast and settled down watching his float. After a minute or two he turned to see if Billy was coming back to fish and saw him collapsed on the ground, still holding his hands to his chest. He ran over. Billy was gasping for air, unable to move. He cradled Billy's head in his lap, tears pouring down his face, his mouth trying to form words. Billy passed out.

Andy didn't know what was happening but he knew he had to get help. He looked frantically around for somebody, but the two anglers had long since disappeared to the far end of the lake. He gently lowered Billy's head to the ground and ran off.

Andy hared through the woods. He tripped over a tree root and fell. He jumped up and ran on. Suddenly he saw two teenagers on motor-bikes, slaloming in and out of the trees, their tyres throwing up arcs of dirt and leaves. Andy ran towards them, waving his arms. The bikers were trying to outride each other and were moving fast and erratically. One of them nearly ran Andy down and pulled to a halt. When he saw Andy looking distressed he accelerated away as fast as he could, followed closely by his mate. Andy waved desperately at them to come back but they were soon out of sight.

Andy ran towards a small unsurfaced road. Through a gap in the trees he could see a car coming. He tried to run even faster, grunting and waving his arms, but the car had jolted past before he reached the road. He stood, looking up and down the road, almost exhausted and in a state of shock. The road was very quiet. He ran back into the wood.

On a path through the woods an old man was exercising his four dogs. Andy came running up and the dogs jumped about him, barking excitedly. Andy grabbed the old man's legs and clung to them.

'Whoa . . . whoa up there.' The old man prised Andy away from his legs. 'Now . . . what's the matter?'

Andy got hold of the old man's hand and pulled him along with all his strength.

'All right, boy, I'm coming.'

The small procession, Andy leading the old man at a trot and the four dogs running as a pack, moved towards the lake and Billy.

TWENTY-ONE

CONNIE and Vin sat in the hospital waiting room. Billy was in a special heart unit and they waited, pale and silent, for news. Ray came in and sat beside Connie.

'How is he?'

'We won't know for a while,' she said. 'He's in the emergency cardiac unit.'

'What happened?'

'He'd taken Andy fishing . . .'

Vin looked at his brother.

'While Reen and I went to the school.'

At home, Renie was coping as best she could. The doctor had been in to give Andy a sedative. She was sitting by his bedside while he slept, exhausted after the traumas of the morning. The curtains were drawn, though it was still light, when Sammy poked her head round the door.

'Mum?' she whispered.

Renie turned, putting a finger to her lips. She got up and slipped out of the room. Karen was also on the landing. Both the girls sensed something was wrong and looked questioningly at their mother.

'He's all right,' Renie reassured them.

'Why did the doctor come, then?' Sammy asked.

'Just to make sure.'

'Is something wrong, Mum?' Karen asked.

'Grandpop's not very well.'

'Is he in bed?'

'I'll explain later. Go and get yourselves something to eat, I'll be down in a minute.'

'Where's Dad?'

'He's all right. Just do as you're told, I'll be down in a minute.'

Renie shooed them downstairs and went back into Andy's room.

Joey was looking for a fare when he heard another cab hooting behind him. It overtook, forcing Joey into the kerb, and Griff jumped out and ran to talk to Joey through the open window.

'Am I glad I found you!'

'You look like a rat's run up your trousers!'

'It's Billy!'

Joey was immediately serious. 'What about him?'

Griff spoke urgently. 'He's had a heart attack. He's in hospital, out in the sticks. He's bad, Joey!'

Phil stood on the steps leading down to the basement flat. The house was run down, with paint peeling off the woodwork, a window broken and repaired with hardboard. Phil walked down the steps, rang the doorbell and waited. The door opened and Lowe looked at him.

'Yes?' Lowe said.

Phil didn't know how the workman who'd identified him to the police would react. He faced Lowe in the doorway.

'Who are you? What do you want?'

Phil realised with amazement that Lowe had no idea who he was. He improvised. 'Er, is it Mr Lowe?'

'That's right.'

'You do roofs?'

'I do all sorts.'

'I've, er, I've just bought a house,' Phil said. 'Needs a bit doing to it. I wonder if you could give me a quote for roof repairs?'

'Where? What's the address, is it local?'

'I'll write it down for you – and my telephone number.' He made a show of searching for a pen. 'Have you got a pen or something?'

'Better come in.' Lowe held the door open. He led the way into a small basement room. 'You got anyone else quoting?'

'No. No, I haven't.' Phil glanced around. Lowe clearly lived alone. One wall had a large framed picture of the Queen, beside it a smaller framed picture of the Royal Family. Lowe rummaged in a drawer for a biro and a pad and sat at the table.

'Spend half the morning on your roof, then someone undercuts you,' he grumbled. 'Waste of time, could be working, earning. What's your name?'

'Fox. Philip Fox,' Phil said coldly.

Lowe began to write. 'Mister Fox . . .'

The name suddenly clicked. He looked up.

'That's right,' Phil said. 'You didn't know who I was, did you?'

'You better get out of here!' Lowe stood up.

'Yesterday you gave the police a detailed description of me, signed a statement. Now I'm standing three feet away and you don't know me from Adam!'

'You get out of here or I'll sling you out.'

'I'm violent, dangerous, assault people. I wouldn't bet the rent on your chances.' Phil said ironically.

'I'll ring the police.' Lowe went to the phone.

'You do that,' Phil bluffed. 'I've got a few questions I want to ask you. They might be very interested in the answers.'

Lowe's hand came away from the receiver. Now Phil was sure he'd got him.

'I don't want trouble,' Lowe said uncertainly.

'You've *got it*, old son.'

'I know your sort.'

'My *sort*?'

'Lefty boot boys!'

'Oh, that's a new one. "Lefty boot boys." You know, Mr Lowe, you have a definite poetic potential.'

Phil's sarcasm got Lowe going.

'Hard-working, decent people pay their taxes to send Trotsky rubbish like you to our universities. It's criminal, bloody disgrace.'

'Hard-working, decent people . . .' Phil paused. 'Like you?'

'That's right, you clever bastard. Like me and millions more, paying to keep parasites, political perverts like you! If you don't like it here, why don't you bugger off – Moscow, Peking – see how you like it there. You wouldn't last two minutes, they'd stick you up against a wall and shoot you!'

'I don't have to ask your politics, do I?'

'I love my country and my Queen and I don't care who knows it. But your sort could never understand that. All you want to do is disrupt, undermine everything. Anyone who loves this country is a fascist to you, you're warped. I'm not a fascist, I'm not National Front, I'm an Englishman, a patriot and bloody proud of it.'

Phil looked at him and spoke slowly.

'A worker, a tax-payer, a patriot . . . and a liar!'

'You get out of here!'

'Who gave you my description to take to the police?'

'I saw you. I was up on that roof and I saw *you* throw that bottle at Mr Leeson. A man like that, attacked, assaulted by a mob of perverts. Kicked and spat on, a gentleman like that. A bloody outrage! And you organised it.'

'Who told you that?'

Lowe was suddenly on guard. 'The police!'

'No, they didn't.'

'I heard it.'

'Where from?'

'Somewhere,' Lowe said uncomfortably.

'You mean someone. The same someone who told you I threw that bottle, the same one who told you I'm a trouble-maker, an extremist, told you the only thing to do with *political perverts* like me is to get rid of them.'

'You threw that bottle,' Lowe said desperately.

'No, no I didn't, Mr Lowe,' Phil said quietly. 'And what's more, you know I didn't.'

'I'd like to see you prove that.'

Phil decided to carry his bluff through.

'I don't have to.' He turned to leave the room.

'What do you mean?' Lowe came after him. 'I asked you a question!'

Phil stopped at the door. 'The student who did throw that bottle has come forward.'

'You're lying . . .' Lowe wasn't sure. 'Bloody liar!'

'It's going to make your statement look a bit sick.'

'But . . . they, but they said . . .'

'They?'

'You go to hell!' Lowe said.

'Giving a false statement to the police is a very serious offence,' Phil baited him.

'Get out!'

'Rushmer, was it . . . and Leal?' Lowe reacted in spite of himself and Phil saw it. 'Those two well-known blue-arsed Tory tigers? That figures, they hate me just enough to try something like this.'

'I don't know what you're talking about.' Lowe pushed Phil to the door.

'What did they tell you – that an independent witness would carry more weight?'

Lowe snatched open the front door. 'You threw it.' Now he

was desperately trying to convince himself. 'You threw that bottle.'

'I think you'd better phone the police and try and explain before it's too late.'

Lowe pushed Phil out and slammed the door.

'They lied to you, Mr Lowe,' Phil called through the door. 'They're using you. You're just as much a victim as I am.'

Phil walked quickly away from the house. He knew he was playing a very dodgy old game.

Vin and Ray were in the hospital waiting room when Joey came in.

'You took your bloody time,' Vin said edgily.

'How is he?'

'Connie's in with him now,' Ray said. 'He's still in the emergency unit.'

'I've sent Kenny a cable,' Vin said. 'He'll be on the first plane back.'

'Couldn't you phone?'

'I did. They were out. I told him to phone Renie, tell us what flight.'

'I'll meet them,' Joey said. 'What about Phil?'

Ray frowned. 'Connie says he's in town. Billy went to see him at his bird's place. We've got the address but the bloody phone number's ex-directory.'

Connie came in, looking exhausted. Joey put his arm round her and gave her a kiss and a squeeze.

'Hello, Joey,' she said wanly.

'He's a tough old bird, Mum, he'll be dancin' in two weeks' time.'

'What did the specialist say?' Vin asked.

Connie sighed. 'We just have to wait, Vin.' She managed a brief, brave smile. 'It's all so sudden. One minute he's there, beside you, the next . . . I never ever really thought about this sort of day.'

Kenny and Nan approached the desk of their Spanish hotel. They were relaxed and happy after a night out. Nan was looking beautiful in a long white dress that showed off her tan.

'Where was it he said he was from?' Nan asked.

'The Yank?'

'Something "Needle".' She laughed.

'Washakie Needle . . . Wyoming!'

Kenny turned to the Spanish desk clerk.

'Twenty-six please.'

The clerk got their key. He took Vin's cable from the pigeon-hole. 'A cable for you, sir. There was a telephone call earlier.'

Kenny took it.

'I hope it's not Eddie again,' Nan said.

'Probably got me another fight lined up,' Kenny joked.

He opened the cable and read it. 'It's Pop.' Kenny gave the cable to Nan. He turned to the clerk. 'I want two seats on the first plane back to England.' Nan read the cable. She couldn't help starting to cry. Kenny put his arm round her.

'It's very difficult, sir.' The desk clerk was trying to be helpful in his bureaucratic way. 'The time of night. You will have to wait . . .'

'Look, just get us on the first flight out. I don't care what it costs . . . just *do it*.'

Ray came up to the door of Anna's flat, checked the number and rang the bell. Anna opened the door.

'Are you Anna?'

'Yes?'

'Is Phil here? I'm his brother, Ray.'

'I thought he would be.'

'Any idea where he is?'

'No.'

'It's very important.'

'Come in,' Anna said.

Ray walked in and Anna closed the door.

'Maybe he just hasn't come in yet?'

'No . . . his bag's not here.'

'Has he gone back to college?' Ray suggested.

'I only left a couple of hours ago. If he had gone back I'd have seen him.'

'I've got to find him,' Ray said grimly.

Rushmer's room was in darkness when he let himself in. He'd been drinking and fumbled with his keys, throwing them on to a

'They all love you, Billy.'

Billy's mind was wandering. 'Where's Phil?' he asked again.

'He'll be here soon, love.'

'Good boys, my boys . . . my sons. God blessed me with a fine family . . . Where's Phil?' He looked past Connie to Kenny. 'Is that Phil? That you, son?'

Connie glanced up at the nurse, who made a sign that they should leave soon.

'Clever little devil . . . proud of him,' Billy was saying.

Phil drove like a madman, cutting in and out of the traffic lanes. He didn't even hear the other drivers hooting him. He tried to force more speed from the car, hammering on the wheel in frustration. He had a terrible premonition that time was against him. He missed his turning a couple of times, not knowing the area. He suddenly saw the sign for the hospital pointing back the way he'd just come. He slammed on the brakes and did a squealing U-turn, mounting the pavement on the opposite side before bumping down and accelerating back up the road. At the hospital he jumped out of the car, abandoning it to run into the entrance hall. He quickly found a nurse to direct him and ran through the long, echoing corridors.

Inside the waiting room, the whole family was grouped around Connie. They seemed strangely composed, as for a formal portrait. Connie was very still, the only one seated. Her face was white as ivory. She was serene, controlling her grief. Phil stopped. No one spoke, but every eye was on him. He stood quite still, apart from the gathered family, like the stranger Pop had accused him of being. He knew that he was too late. King Billy was dead. Nothing would ever be the same again.

shelf by the door. He switched on the light.

'Been celebrating, Rushmer?' Phil's voice came from behind him. Rushmer swivelled round to face him.

'How did you get in here?'

'Through the door.' Phil pointed.

'It was locked.'

'Was it?' Phil asked innocently.

Rushmer swayed on his feet.

'You broke into my room!'

'You better sit down before you fall down.'

'Get out of my room,' Rushmer said, suddenly aggressive.

'Don't get silly . . . I'm just itching to bang you.'

'What do you want?'

'I've had a very informative little chat with your working class friend, Mr Lowe. Tax-payer, patriot and Englishman. He called me a political pervert . . . I seem to have heard that somewhere before?'

Rushmer moved towards the door, but Phil hooked a finger in his jacket collar and pulled him back. He lost his balance and fell over. Phil looked down at him.

'I haven't finished.'

Rushmer covered up as if he expected Phil to kick him.

'I wouldn't touch you with a disinfected stick,' Phil said disgustedly.

Rushmer staggered to his feet and slumped on to his bed.

'I feel sick.' He put a hand to his head.

'You *are* sick. How long do you think Lowe will last in court?'

'The inquiry has been dropped.'

'No thanks to you,' Phil said. 'I bet Leeson didn't know what you were up to, what your little game was, did he? Or the UCA?'

From Rushmer's face he could see he was right. 'It would have been very embarrassing for them.' Phil paused. 'No. I'm talking about when I sue Lowe for making that statement . . . and you for conspiracy!'

'You wouldn't dare. You couldn't prove anything.'

Phil turned and walked to the door. 'See you in court.'

He opened the door. Rushmer panicked. 'Come back!'

Phil turned slowly.

'Let's . . . let's talk about this . . . mix-up,' Rushmer faltered.

'Let's,' said Phil.

*

Femi ran up the stairs of Phil's lodging-house. He tried Phil's door but it was locked. He knocked and waited, knocked again.

'Phil?' he called through the door. 'Phil, are you there?'

He took a notebook from his pocket, got out a pen and printed a note.

URGENT. YOUR FATHER IS ILL. PLEASE RING ANNA IN LONDON IMMEDIATELY. FEMI.

Femi tore the page out of the book and stuck it between the door and the frame so that Phil would see it when he came back.

When Phil got back to his room it was very late. He'd had a long day, ending with another talk with Detective Sergeant Poyzer. He was tired when he unlocked his door and didn't see the note from Femi, which had fallen to the floor. He went straight to bed and fell asleep.

It was the early hours of the morning when Femi and Don came by the house to check that Phil had got the message. At the door to Phil's room Femi saw the note on the floor and picked it up. They walked into the unlocked room and Don shook him awake. A few minutes later Phil came tearing down the stairs, tucking his shirt into his trousers. He jumped into Don's car, started it and accelerated away with a squeal of tyres.

All the Fox family, except Phil, were at the hospital. Joey had collected Kenny and Nan at the airport and Kenny went straight into the cardiac unit with Connie. Billy had regained consciousness but was very weak. Kenny was close to tears when Billy whispered, almost inaudibly. 'Who . . . who's that?'

'It's me, Pop . . . Kenny.' He bent closer.

'You're . . . on holiday?'

'We're back now, Pop. Come to see you.'

Kenny held his father's hands. He couldn't stop the tears.

' 'Ere . . . that's enough of that.'

Connie came close to hear what Billy was saying. He looked at her.

'Where, where's Phil?'

'He's on his way, darling.'

'Good boys. Good boys, our boys,' Billy said to her.